FIVE DAYS

A NOVEL

Matt Micros

For my parents.

Wishing they were still here
and looking forward to a reunion someday so I can
ask my mom why
she owned so many vacuums.

And for Katy.

Who unquestionably made my parents
more comfortable knowing they were leaving me in
good hands.

<u>*Also by Matt Micros*</u>

~The Knights of Redemption ~

~The Chameleon ~

TABLE OF CONTENTS

FIVE DAYS

"Is it a vision, or a waking dream? Fled is that music. Do I wake? Or Sleep?"

John Keats

I

~THE END OF THE BEGINNING ~

The warmth and sun-drenched days of late summer, had been replaced by the cold, darkness of November, where the crisp chill served as a precursor to a winter that would long overstay its welcome once the holidays had past. Students that were eager to learn something new and different back in August had been replaced by unmotivated, and occasionally cruel creatures that were recognizable as human beings only by their DNA.

When the bell sounded signaling the end of another particularly draining day, it was difficult to determine who was happier—the students or the teachers. Mike Postman flipped the Algebra textbook he had been teaching from closed, waved as the students poured from the room, and sat at his desk for the obligatory twenty minutes mandated by the teachers' contract.

Mike looked like he was in his early 30's, but was actually nearly 40, with the sort of generic good looks that enabled him to pass as either the clean-cut boy next door, or a Hollywood character actor. He pulled into the driveway of his modest two-story cottage across the street from one of the oldest beaches in Southwestern Connecticut. On this day, he didn't even go inside, but instead, immediately crossed to where the multi-million dollar homes stood. It wasn't much of a stretch to say that his home could have passed as a guesthouse for any one of them.

Walking on the path that ran along the Connecticut shoreline, Mike bit down his lower lip, the way he frequently did anytime he was thinking. Autumn always had a certain smell to it, he thought; even back when he was a kid. Not a strong one, mind you, but rather a soft, subtle smell, not unlike the gentle scent of a woman's perfume as she walked past. The interesting thing was that autumn smelled differently depending on where you were. In Florence, Italy, autumn was damp and musty, clinging to your senses like a memory you would never forget. In Chicago, autumn smelled like burning leaves. In New York City, it smelled like roasted chestnuts and Italian sausage. And in Woodmont - on - the - Sound, Connecticut, the smell of autumn was crisp and clean, like a freshly laundered shirt.

Gone were the rollerbladers and sunbathers of summer. Weather wise, this day was symbolic of his mood; colder than it looked, with clouds battling the blue sky for prominence. As a profession, teaching was simultaneously rewarding and frustrating. On more than one occasion, he had thought about trying something different, but he didn't know what else he was suited to do. Besides, the highs of teaching were generally higher than anything else he could imagine doing. There was nothing quite like seeing the smile of a struggling teenager after you had managed to give them some measure of hope. And yet, for every time he felt as though he was making a difference, something would happen as if to not so gently remind him that just maybe he was wrong about that.

He heard the faint shout of a little boy as he came around the bend. Barely audible at first, he was so entrenched in thought, he didn't even notice at first. But it grew louder with each successive shout, as a boy of about ten approached him frantically.

"Mister! Mister! My friend just fell in off the pier and he can't swim! I'm not good enough to pull him out! Please help!"

Mike didn't hesitate, throwing his jacket onto the ground and kicking off his shoes as he ran to the end of the pier and dove in headfirst. It was abundantly clear that he wasn't a strong swimmer himself, but after a few awkward strokes, he managed to reach the boy.

Holding him around his neck with his right hand gripping the boy's shirt collar, he dragged him along, struggling to keep himself above water in the process. With the other boy lying prone on the pier with an outstretched arm, Mike swung around and tried throwing the boy toward the arm. Once he saw that the boy's friend had grabbed him and helped lift him onto the pier, Mike relaxed, and then suddenly, and yet almost peacefully, plunged beneath the surface of the water. For the briefest of moments, he felt himself taking in water--through his nose, mouth, and ears. His eyes were burning from the salt water. His lungs felt as though they were about to explode. And then he felt *nothing* at all.

When he came to, he found himself lying amongst a bevy of soft, white, puffy, cumulus clouds. He staggered to his feet just in time to see a tram, not unlike one you might find at Disney World, approaching in the far off distance. It seemed to make up several miles in a few moments, before it eased to a stop directly in front of him.

"Let's go, Mike. Get on," the driver said impatiently.

"Where are you going?" he asked.

"You'll know when you get there," was the response.

How did he know him? Where was he? And why was he the youngest one on board by at least 25 years?

The tram tunneled through the clouds, emerging at the front gate of what appeared to be Caesar's Palace. Not the one from ancient Rome, but rather the one that had been modeled after it on the Las Vegas strip.

"This is your stop," the driver said, matter-of-factly, a nod of his head indicating he was supposed to get off.

When no one else moved toward the exit, Mike realized the man was talking to him, and he stepped off the tram.

"How did I end up in Vegas?" he asked no one in particular.

The response came from a voice behind him.

"You didn't," the voice said.

It was a deep, James Earl Jones-like voice.

"I didn't?"

"No. But we had to do something. We were getting too many complaints that our accommodations weren't as nice as those down below. His home looks like Graceland."

The man was African-American, wearing a white, flowing gown that was a cross between a priest's robe and a Roman toga.

"Elvis lives downstairs?" Mike asked in a perpetual state of disbelief and confusion.

"Of course not," the man laughed. "Elvis is a music teacher in Wisconsin."

Mike nodded as if this somehow made sense. "Then who's down below?" he asked.

"Beelzebub. Satan. You probably know him more readily as the devil."

"So if he's downstairs, then that must mean I'm in..."

The man nodded. "Gabriel--at your service."

"How did I end up here, Gabriel?"

"You died saving that little boy's life. Or should I say—you *let* yourself die."

"I don't really recall that much about it," Mike responded, "And I don't mean that in a Bill Clintonesque sort of way."

"Your memory will come back a little at a time as you need it," Gabriel assured him.

Mike glanced around him and nodded at an elderly couple that walked past. They didn't even acknowledge him.

"If this is heaven, Gabriel, how come no one's very friendly?"

"Oh, they're not going to be friendly to you, Mike."

"Why not?" he asked, offended.

Gabriel stopped walking—took on a more serious tone now. "Because you took your own life, while most of these people has theirs taken away from them."

He decided not to waste too much time thinking about it. He simply had too many questions that needed to be answered.

"Then why am I here, if I'm such a bad guy?"

"Did I say you were a bad guy?"

"You implied as much."

"Don't read too much into things," Gabriel answered, his tone much more cordial once again. "And you're here because you're visiting."

"I'm visiting?"

Mike didn't much care for the sound of that.

"Is this some sort of a tryout?" he followed up with.

Mike had always hated tryouts. It didn't matter whether it was an athletic team, the school play, or a job interview. He wanted to be wanted. He didn't want to have to convince someone he was good enough.

"Of course not."

"So after I visit, then what?"

"Then you go back."

"Then I go back," Mike repeated.

"Do you always repeat everything people say to you?" Gabriel asked.

"Only when I think they're full of..."

He stopped himself just short of finishing his sentence. He thought better of it, considering his surroundings, and also how tenuous his tenure there appeared to be.

"So I get to go back where?" he continued.

"To where you came from.   To any year you like actually.   You've been given a great gift, Mike. You've been given the opportunity to go back and relive any five days from your life of your own choosing."

"And why exactly do I get to do that?"

"Have you ever wished you had the chance to do something over? To go back knowing then what you know now?"

"Of course. Doesn't everyone?"

"Well, you have the opportunity to do that."

"Does everyone get to go back?"

"Not everyone," Gabriel answered cryptically.

"Then why me?"

"It will all be explained to you in time.   But we really need to get going."

With that, Gabriel smiled a knowing smile and held the casino door open for him to enter. Mike bit down on his lower lip as they walked past the cavalcade of high-end shops just inside the entrance, while the distant chiming of slot machines and occasional screams of joy echoed down the corridor.

"So, Gabriel," Mike said with a wink, "do they have any ten dollar craps tables at this time of day?"

"We don't use money to gamble up here."

"Then what do you use? Cars? Clothes? Women?" He winked again, and made a clicking sound with his tongue.

"People gamble for the thrill of beating the system," he answered simply.

"Don't you think it would add an additional thrill

if a cool grand was riding on one toss of the dice?"

"It wouldn't matter. People have no use for money here. Everything is already provided for them. Food, clothing, shelter, entertainment, transportation..."

"Sounds like a communist block nation. Well, if they don't need money, what would be the incentive to work?"

"Most people don't. Most people have worked their entire lives and are glad not to have to any longer."

"But then how does anything get done?"

He rethought his question as soon as the words left his mouth. After all, it was heaven.

"Some people choose to work anyway."

"Why would anyone *choose* to work?" Mike asked. It was a concept he had a difficult time wrapping his arms around. Most days, he had come home so exhausted both mentally and physically, that he wasn't sure he would be able to do it again 12 hours later. Of course he always had, but if anyone had given him a choice, he would have gladly chosen to follow the Mets around the country instead.

"You yourself once said that if you won the lottery, you would still work, only without having to worry about money, you'd take a job where you really felt as though you could make a difference."

"How do you know I said that?" Mike asked. It was true. He had said it. But he was trying to impress a girl at the time and thought it sounded better than drinking beer, following the Mets and playing Xbox.

"I know everything there is to know about you,

Mike. Except for one thing."

    "And what's that?"

    "All in good time, my friend," Gabriel said as they continued down the narrowing corridor.

II

~THE RECOVERY ROOM~

"*Y*ou know, I think you're right. I'd prefer not to work after all," Mike said.

"And why's that?" Gabriel asked, curious now.

"Well, I don't think you'd have the kind of job I'd want up here. Besides, being a pro basketball player would lose some of its luster if I had to take an 85 year old to the hole."

"I could see how it might."

In just a few dozen steps, they had managed to make the chiming from the casino a distant memory. They continued down a hallway with dozens of closed doors. There were no numbers, no names, on any of them.

"The only other job I'd consider is working with kids. Not as a teacher, but like a counselor or something. But I haven't seen any kids up here."

"Kids are in a different place."

"A better place?"

"A different place."

"Do they get to go back?"

"Some of them."

"You're kind of evasive in your answers,

Gabriel."

Gabriel smiled as he held open a door at the very end of the corridor. "As are you."

The room was tastefully decorated in burgundies and tans, with cherry oak trim, oriental rugs, and seven leather home theatre seats that faced a wall covered by velvet curtains that ran from ceiling to floor.

"Is this like a screening room or something?" Mike asked. "The angels get together here for movie night?"

"It's a recovery room actually."

"Recovery from what?"

"From yourself."

Mike was getting a bit irritated. "Look, if this is about why I killed myself, I already told you I don't know why I did it. Everything's a blur."

"That's what this room is for. To help you recover your memory." Gabriel continued speaking in a calm, almost measured tone. He was handling Mike, but at least Mike knew it. "Can I get you something to drink?"

"You got any Corona?"

"I was thinking more along the lines of orange juice."

"No, thanks," Mike answered before he noticed Gabriel pouring what appeared to be the tallest, freshest, coolest glass of orange juice he had ever seen. "On second thought..."

Gabriel had held it out for him before he had even changed his mind.

"This isn't some sort of truth serum is it?"

"No, it's just orange juice," Gabriel laughed.

"Will it still give me the runs? It always used to give me the runs on earth."

"I don't think you'll have to worry about that. He motioned toward one of the chairs. Have a seat."

The lights dimmed and the curtains opened, revealing a wall size window that looked down into a church. It was a funeral. Mike's funeral. Every seat in every pew was filled the way it was anytime someone died young and unexpectedly. His parents, sister and brother-in-law were in the front. They didn't have any tears left to cry, and looked like they hadn't slept in days. What appeared to be hundreds of his current and former students were in varying degrees of disarray, although from his vantage point, it was difficult to make out who was who.

He had always wondered what it would be like to attend his own funeral. To see who came. To see how people reacted. To see what they really thought of him. He supposed everyone had those same thoughts, but he was actually getting to do it. It wasn't at all what he expected. It was as if they were watching the service from the balcony. Mike stood and walked closer to the window, close enough to touch it, scanning the scene below without so much as a word.

Gabriel handed him a remote control. "Go ahead. Zoom in. It operates just like a camera."

Mike pointed it at the wall and zoomed in and down on the service.

"Per the family's request, we have a number of people who have stories to share about Mike. Some funny. Some sad. All should help paint the portrait of who he was and what he stood for. We hope that you will listen and enjoy a glimpse into his life," the priest said as a man made his way to the podium.

The man was in his late-forties, handsome, athletic, composed. Mike didn't recognize him at first, but as he zoomed in closer and mentally shaved away the man's mustache and colored his greying hair, he saw his childhood friend. As the man began to speak, Mike felt his legs go weak and fell backwards into the chair.

* * *

"Mike Postman was my neighbor growing up. I was his sister's age—five years older than him, but he and I quickly became the best of friends out of our love of sports. As the "unofficial leader" on a street full of kids, I was the one who organized the games of football, basketball, soccer, baseball and softball.

Mike was about eight or nine when he first started playing with us, and back then, we used to make sure he was always on the winning team. Someone would fumble the ball on purpose, or slip when they went to tackle him, but he caught on quickly, and he soon demanded that everyone play it straight. Mike was an unusual nine-year old. He never cried when he lost. He never whined that the teams were unfair. And he never complained when someone tackled him hard.

I like to think that in many ways, Mike became a better athlete when he was older in large part to playing with us as a kid. If no one else was around, Mike and I played individual sports like home run derby and golf. If I only had a dime for every window we broke back then, I would be a rich man today. When the weather was bad and we couldn't play outside, Mike and I played Sports Illustrated's baseball and football board games. I was an Orioles fan. He liked the Mets. We must have replayed the '69 World Series a hundred times, and as in real life, the Amazins must have won 90 of them. We were both Cowboys fans during a time when it was good to be a Cowboys fan. Roger Staubach. Drew Pearson. Ed "Too Tall" Jones. Thomas "Hollywood" Henderson. Two close losses to the Steelers in the Super Bowl, and finally—victory over the Denver Broncos. I was in college at that point. And although we had lost touch by then, Mike was the person I thought of when the final whistle blew.

As the years passed, we kept up with each other through our mothers. It seemed as though we were living parallel lives. He went to college in the Midwest days after I moved back to Connecticut. I moved to Florida two weeks after he left Florida for Los Angeles. Every few years, we would catch up during the holidays at a party or on the phone, and it seemed as though we had seen each other only the day before. I had always considered him to be the little brother I had always wanted but didn't have. But I always wondered how he had viewed me. It would be 25 years before I would find out.

About five years ago, I received a manila envelope in the mail from my mother one morning. Inside was a chapter from a book Mike had written simply entitled, "David". The last paragraph will stay with me forever.

David taught me how to play every sport I've ever played. Football. Basketball. Baseball. Even sports he wasn't even as familiar with like soccer. He taught me poise and composure by giving me confidence.   He's the reason I teach today.   I remember hearing his parents and my parents talk about how David was never motivated to do his schoolwork.   To me, he was already a teacher without even knowing it. He shaped my personality. The one who taught me patience in dealing with little kids. He was a dreamer they said. My parents said I was just like him.   It was the greatest compliment they could give me. For to me, David was a hero, and it is because of him that I will always think that the world looks like a much nicer place when viewed through the eyes of a nine year old.

To this day, that chapter remains simply, the greatest honor I have ever received."

* * *

The man stepped away from the podium to make way for a beautiful woman. Tall and thin, with shortish, straight brown hair and crystal clear, sparkling blue eyes, Mike recognized Jordan Roberts immediately.

* * *

"I first met Mike when I was in sixth grade," she began. "He was the lone freshman on the Varsity soccer team that my older brother was the Captain of. Mike was so shy and little back then, it was hard to imagine that just three years later, he would replace my brother as the big-shot, senior Captain. I had entered high school at that point, and although he and I had barely spoken in three years, Mike had this way of making you feel as though you were among his closest friends after a few short moments. He did it partly by making you laugh at his outrag-

eous comments. Sometimes he did it by telling you something personal about his life that made you feel special. But usually he did it by taking the time to listen to things no one cared to listen to.

I had a lot of problems my freshman year. My older brother was off at college, and my father was battling what is now known as "clinical depression." Back then, they didn't have the drugs available to treat it that they do now, so my father found himself in and out of the hospital on more than one occasion. He was finally released for good, or so we hoped, a few days before Christmas of that year. But what looked to be a happy occasion, turned tragic when my mother and I walked into our living room one night and found my father had shot himself to death.

I didn't know how to react at the time. I only knew I didn't want to be alone. So I went into school the very next morning. Most people hadn't heard about it yet, and the ones that did were walking on eggshells around me. But not Mike. When he arrived that day, he walked up behind me, and threw his shoulder into my back, and sent my books flying across the floor. I remember hearing a collective gasp from everyone else, wondering what my reaction would be. As I turned to face him he said, "What? You got a problem? Cause I'll knock you out if you do."

I laughed, and everyone breathed a sigh of relief. He clearly didn't know I remember thinking to myself. "My father killed himself last night," I said to him at last.

"I know. I'm so sorry, Jord," he said as he

*helped me pick up my books and walked me down
the hall.*

*Some people go their whole lives without ever
knowing what to say in a crisis. Mike, however, was
one of those people who was able to say or do the
perfect thing by blending humor with sincerity.*

*Until I heard what happened to him the other
day, I hadn't seen or spoken to him in more than
twenty years, but I thought about him from time to
time. And every now and then when I was having a
bad day, I found myself wishing he was around to
make me laugh.*

* * *

Another female approached. By the smiles and
nods that were exchanged, it appeared that the two
women knew each other. Blaire Kaanen could have
been the head of the PTA or the director of an art
museum; maybe both.

* * *

*"I transferred into Mike's high school my junior
year, not knowing a soul before I got there. As is
usually the case, none of the girls were very nice to
me at first, and although most of the guys were, I
didn't take that as much of a compliment since they
would have flocked to any new girl just because they
were new. So I pretty much kept to myself for the
first month or so, until the lunch tables changed and
I ended up at Mike's table.*

*The lunch system was set so that every teacher
was assigned a rotating table of nine students. In
addition, there were two student-only tables that were
run by the student government. Mike was in charge
of one of those tables. I had heard of him prior to*

that—which is to say I knew he was a good athlete, and a good student—but I had never actually met him until the day I was assigned to his table.

"Who's this little tramp?" were the first words he ever spoke to me.

I felt my jaw hit the floor from shock.

For Mike, that was the same as saying hello.

"Say outrageous things all the time, and people assume you're joking, even when you're not. It helps you get away with things," he would later explain.

And so it went. He would see me in the hall, punch me in the arm a few times, and call me a "whorebag" or a "slut" or something of that nature. I loved the fact that Mike was the only person who could make me laugh even when I was having the worst possible day.

Our relationship must have seemed pretty confusing to an outsider, but we actually became close friends. In fact, there was a time where it looked like we might become more than that, but I was still involved in an extremely unhealthy relationship that I couldn't break free from. Faced with a choice between someone completely right for me, and someone completely wrong, I naturally chose completely wrong.

"Typical female," Mike said. "Always want what you can't or shouldn't have."

He was right of course, but that was a lesson I wouldn't learn until many years later when faced with a similar choice. This time I chose correctly--except my husband never calls me a "whorebag", "slut", or "little tramp". At least not to my face anyway."

* * *

Mike smiled as she spoke. Some people, no matter the time that has past or the distance between you, would always have a special place in your heart. An older man was next. Early 60's, his once dark hair now white. His walk, at one time a pace with which everyone struggled to keep up with, had slowed to a comfortable stroll.

* * *

"Every coach, no matter the level or the sport, will try to convince you they don't play favorites. But the truth of the matter is that their favorites are those players who show up on time, ready to work just as hard at practice as they would in a game. Players whose smart play and positive attitude make you feel like a good coach.

For me, Mike Postman was my favorite for all of those reasons and more. I was his Junior Varsity basketball coach his freshman year of high school. Mike had a terrific handle, and could breakdown just about any press. He wasn't the greatest pure shooter I'd ever seen, but he had incredible balance and the ability to hit off balance shots in traffic when you needed them the most. What separated him from others like him, however, was his refusal to lose. He would do whatever it took to win; dive 20 feet across the floor for a loose ball, race back to break up a fast break, or mix it up inside for a key rebound even though he was barely 5'8. In fact, it was on one of those occasions that he caught an elbow, breaking his nose and giving him a slight concussion in the process. Somehow, he managed to convince me at halftime that he was ready to go back in. He ended up breaking two fingers on his shooting hand in the second half. But he never let on until after the game was over. Three days later, he was back playing with the Varsity team in the state tournament.

At the end of the season, the Varsity coach resigned and I was named the new head coach with the opportunity to coach Mike for three more years. But somewhere between March of his sophomore year and November of his junior year, there was a noticeable change in his attitude. The school had always had a policy enabling multi-sport athletes to take a week off between seasons that overlapped, but until his junior year, Mike had never before exercised that option. My initial reaction was that he was just burned out from a tough soccer season, and the beginning pressure of searching for colleges. But once rumors began to circulate that he wasn't going to play at all, I went over to see him.

He explained that he was burnt out and didn't want to play. I kept thinking all the accolades he had received in soccer had made him less interested in basketball, but that once the regular season rolled around, his competitive juices would begin flowing and he would be back. I was wrong.

I think his plan all along was to come back out for his senior year when he and his friends would comprise most of the team. What he hadn't counted on was his parents informing him that unless he got his way back onto the team as a junior, there would be no senior year.

He called me at home one night with about three weeks left in the season. It must have taken an awful lot of pride swallowing for him to make the call. He explained that he made a mistake, and wanted to

*apologize to the team, but mostly to me. I told him
he had it wrong and that it was the team he owed the
apology to. I also told him it would be up to them
whether or not we took him back.*

*It was a split vote. His friends on the team all
wanted him back. The seniors didn't. I broke the
tie in his favor. Seven weeks to the day he had quit,
and after just one practice, he suited up for a game. I
think Mike's plan was to pay his dues for the
remainder of the season. Work hard in practice and
sit quietly at the end of the bench during games. But
I thought that would have been letting him off too
easy. Four minutes into his first game back with the
team, I sent him in. He had a look of panic on his
face when I called his name. And you could have
heard a pin drop in the crowd when I made him
stand up. He wanted no part of going in over
players that had been there for the last two months.
And that's exactly why I sent him in.*

*Some people criticized me for what they claimed
was a win-at-all-costs attitude. But the plain and
simple truth was that our basketball team that year
wasn't very good with or without Mike on the floor.
And sure, there are times when I look back and
wonder if I did the right thing by playing him so
soon. But then I think about how the two minutes
Mike Postman spent at the scorer's table that night
waiting to go in, might very well have been the
loneliest two minutes of his life."*

* * *

"Was he right?" Gabriel asked.

Mike nodded. "Coach was always right. I
probably learned more about accountability in those

two minutes than I did the rest of my years combined."

"Was he the reason you became a teacher?"

"Teaching wasn't really something I had planned on doing."

"You know what I find interesting? All that time you spent working with kids, and yet, you never had any of your own."

"You see, your boss made it so that you kind of need the cooperation of the opposite sex for that to happen."

"And how do you know it wouldn't have?"

"I don't know that I guess."

"Then why did you quit?"

"I didn't quit on anything," Mike said defensively.

"What about the kids you worked with? You don't think you quit on them?"

"If there's one thing I learned while teaching, it's that kids are resilient. You could be their best friend one day, and they'll forget all about you the next. I don't blame them for it, mind you. I'm sure I was the same way."

"You don't really believe that or you wouldn't have walked away from your job at the talent agency in Los Angeles to teach and coach," Gabriel said.

Mike absently rose to his feet and bit down on his lower lip again. "Don't really know why I did that," he began, before pausing to answer his own question. "Working at the agency was a real hoot and a half—for a while. But then I realized it wasn't brain surgery. I mean, who gives a crap if some idiot movie star has a trailer to work out of that could fit most of Manhattan inside it? It was thrilling meeting famous people at first, but eventually I came to the realization that they were just as full of—crap—as anyone else."

"And so you left to teach."

"It's a little more complicated than that. My dad got sick back east. I had a job lined up in New York City, but it fell through just before I was supposed to move. Teaching seemed to be the logical choice. I wasn't qualified for much else. So, you see, it didn't exactly fall out as nobly as it might have appeared."

"You sell yourself short," Gabriel answered.

"I am short," Mike responded with a wink.

Gabriel was beginning to realize his job might just be considerably more difficult than he originally thought.

"How you ended up teaching is of little consequence," Gabriel assured him. "What you did with it is what matters."

"I'm afraid I didn't do much."

"You helped out a number of kids, whether it be in the classroom, on the athletic fields, or just by listening," Gabriel said.

"It didn't always feel like it," Mike answered. "And I guess after a while it became a little overwhelming."

Mike found Gabriel's lack of response to be some sort of condemnation.

"What? You don't agree?" he asked quickly.

"I didn't say anything," Gabriel responded.

"It's what you didn't say."

"Listen, Mike. I'm not here to judge you. I'm simply trying to find out why you took your own life."

"You know everything else about me. Why is it you don't know why I did what I did?"

"Because the greatest gift mankind was given was free will. Freedom to choose as you please. And although I was well aware of the consequences that might follow a particular choice you made, I had no way of knowing why you made that choice. You're the only one who knows that."

"And if it's not a good enough reason, I don't get to go back, is that it?"

"You get to go back regardless," Gabriel answered. "You get to go back because you saved that little boy's life, and the fact that you took your own in the process, certainly doesn't erase that fact."

Mike turned away again. "Would you believe me if I told you I don't know why I did it? Every day, people wonder what it would be like to throw themselves in front of a bus. Or to drive off a cliff. And for no other reason than to wonder what it would be like. What would happen? Would you survive? What would you find on the other side? You cannot tell me I'm the only person to ever have those thoughts."

"Certainly not," Gabriel said, "But most people have the sense not to act on them."

"I've got a question for you. Every day, innocent people die for no apparent reason. Children. Heroes. Wonderful people who would have contributed so much to society. Why?" Mike demanded.

"You're referring to Kylie?"

"Her and others like her."

"You really liked her, didn't you?"

"You're not answering my question," Mike pressed.

"It's not as simple as all that."

"And why isn't it?" Mike asked as he turned back towards him. "When you take someone's life, it certainly doesn't seem as though they have much choice in the matter. How is that free will?"

"They put themselves in those situations with the choices they made," Gabriel said. "Kylie and her brother drove off a slippery road in the middle of the night."

"Ok. Well, how is that some people who eat right and live right get Cancer, while others smoke like a chimney and live to be 100?"

"Everyone's body makeup is different. Why can some people run faster than others? A catastrophic choice for one person might not affect another at all."

It was a lot to take in and Mike was exhausted. "I don't know what to tell you," he said at last, "maybe I thought my life had reached its pinnacle. That it was never going to get any better. It wasn't a bad life. It was just—just.....ordinary.

III

~THE VIEW FROM THE TOP~

The parade of people to the podium continued as a man about Mike's age approached. Handsome and athletic, with devilish eyes and a warm smile that made women swoon, Eddie Daniels had never been particularly book smart, but had been brilliant in the two ways most necessary to succeed in life. People were drawn to his outgoing and charming personality, but more importantly, he understood people. Knew what they were feeling. Knew what they wanted to hear. Knew how to get them to do what he wanted without them even realizing it.

"I knew Mike for more than 30 years. We first met in elementary school, went to high school together, and then ended up roommates in Los Angeles for seven years. We were east coasters at heart, but there was just something about Southern California. The weather was always gorgeous for starters. I don't think it rained once the first eight months we lived there. And there was always something to do. The beach. Bars. Restaurants. Movie premieres. Pick up basketball games. We

had to continually change jobs because we usually burned up all our sick days for the year by April. We'd inevitably be out watching Monday Night Football—it came on at 6:00pm out there—having a pizza and a pitcher of beer, when one of us would say, "Well, either we order another pitcher, or we head home now. Of course, if we order another pitcher, you know we're out for the night."

I don't think we ever DIDN'T order another pitcher. The next day we'd call in sick and head to the beach. And it would be packed. Mike used to say, "We're idiots who stayed out all night drinking on a weeknight and called in sick. But what are all these other people doing here?" We determined it was because no one in Los Angeles actually works. They either came from old money. New money. Or no money. Wannabee athletes, actors and musicians living way beyond their means. We were hardly ones to talk. In addition to our rented beach house, Mike and I both drove BMW's and I think our combined incomes barely reached six figures. But we had learned that the key to the city where there was always someone richer, better looking, or funnier, was to keep up with the Jones'. Who you were had nothing to do with you per se, but more to do with what you drove and where you worked.

I think that's what bothered Mike the most. He didn't want anything to do with a girl who only talked to him because she thought he could somehow help her career, whereas I had no such problem. But that's what made us great friends. Mike was the responsible one who came to pick us up at a bar one *night after we had been out drinking since happy hour; only to have his car totaled when a drunk driver plowed into us from behind at a traffic light. Mike was the one who drove home our other roommate's one night stand, after our roommate had gotten called into work on a Saturday morning. Mike felt so badly for the girl, he bought her breakfast on the way.*

Mike was the last of the nice guys. A true friend. The voice of reason when things got dicey. As is frequently the case, we've lost touch a bit over the past few years. Our jobs and our families occupy most of our time. But I still think about our friendship. Some people you don't need to see or speak to in order to remain close. If he were here right now, I think he'd agree. I'll miss him."

*   * * **

College girls dig older guys.

That simple phrase was told to us minutes into our freshman year of college by one of the sophomores from down the hall.

"And it won't matter if you were the Captain of the football team, the Homecoming King, or the Student Body President in high school," he continued, "because everyone here was at least one of those. Some were all three. So prepare yourself for a long, dry year just like all of us had as freshmen."

It didn't take long for us to realize that truer words were never spoken. It left us with a choice to make. We could either work hard like all the other lemmings and blend into the ivy and stone building fronts, or we could go the opposite direction

altogether and create personas for ourselves so
ridiculous that we became cartoon-like versions of
our old selves. Of course we chose the latter.

Bobby became the biggest slacker aerospace
engineer in the university. Paul became the biggest
slacker civil engineer. I became the biggest slacker
business major. And Mike became the biggest
slacker Arts and Letters major—which in effect made
him the biggest slacker in the entire university.

The goal wasn't to flunk out. Any idiot could do
that. We wanted to see what we could get away with
not doing. It was from that very principle that the
class cut contest was born. Cut as many classes as
you could while maintaining the highest GPA
possible. The winner would be determined by a
point system. Class cuts times GPA gave you your
total. If you cut 75 classes and had a 2.0, you
received 150 points, while someone who cut 120
classes, but had a 1.0 would only get 120 points.

What began as a close contest turned into a two-
man race between Mike and I by November. Mike
had earned the nickname Pile back in high school,
and when I say earned it, he earned it. It stood for
exactly what you would think. Pile as in Pile of.
About three weeks before the end of the semester,
Pile decided to distance himself from the rest of us
and cut every single class for two weeks straight. He
became so versed in about four different soap operas
that he could have written scripts for any one of
them.

To his credit, it wasn't as easy as it sounds. Notre
Dame had this policy that saw your grade dropped
half a letter for every class you missed more than

three. Pile got around that by striking a deal with his Calculus professor enabling him to miss as many classes as he liked, as long as he kept a "B" average. He made up for it in Latin by treating the professor to lunch in the student center two to three times a week. And in his lecture hall classes, he merely had someone sign him in.

When all was said and done, Pile cut an outrageous 123 out of 150 classes and still managed to pull a 3.0. I came in a distant second with 81 cuts and a 2.9. And thus, the legend of the "Pile" was born. It wasn't an easy reputation to maintain. Constantly having to top his previous exploit. But he certainly did the best he could.

There was the time when he didn't write a term paper for his US Constitution class, but claimed he did, once the doddering, bigoted, crusty old professor handed them back. Keep in mind that this was in the day before personal computers, so no one had backup copies of their papers. The professor thought he had lost the paper and offered to give Pile the same grade he had in the class going in.

*"I was really hoping to raise my grade to a 'B',"
Pile responded. "I spent a lot of time on it."*

He got the "B". You had to give it to him. The guy had balls.

On a different occasion, he decided he wanted to drop his Psychology class because it met too early in the morning. The problem was that his advisor wouldn't let him unless he was in danger of failing it. So Pile became the first person I knew to study for a test so he could fail it. He got a "2", which was really like getting a "98" depending on how you looked at it.

But his true night of greatness occurred when he attempted to drink a case of beer in four hours on a Wednesday night for no other reason than one of the football players had tried and failed. Pile failed too— passing out after number twenty—but somehow managed to make it to his 8am class the following morning. And that, more than anything demonstrated the very essence of the Pile. Cut class all the time, but go to class when no one expected you to.

He wasn't without his failures. There was the time he drove his Criminology professor four hours to the state penitentiary for an optional class trip, only to fail the class anyway. But in the end, I learned some valuable lessons from Pile. Not simply that drinking a case of beer in four hours is nearly impossible to do. But rather, that there is more to an education than what you learn in books and lectures. Twenty years after the fact, I couldn't tell you the name of one of my college professors. What I remember instead are the friendships I made. The things we did. The life-lessons we all learned. Those are the things I remember, not because the other things aren't important, but because interactions with people are more important. The irony of ironies is that one guy who never went to class, the guy who never studied, went on to become a high school teacher.

Mike used to quote from Mark Twain. "An education is what is left after you've forgotten all that you've learned." Of course we might have learned

that a bit sooner had we decided to read that Twain
book in our American Lit class.

* * *

"I've seen enough," Mike said with a wave of his hand.

He walked across the room, clearly agitated.

"Most people enjoy seeing what others have to say about them after they are gone," Gabriel answered.

"I don't enjoy seeing people I care about upset."

"Maybe you should have thought about that before."

"Well, there's not much I can do about that now, is there?" Mike asked rhetorically.

"That's not necessarily true."

Mike began to pace, the wheels in his mind turning at a rapid pace. "So, how does this work?"

"Let me take you to your place, and I'll explain then," Gabriel said.

They took the elevator to the 17th floor of the West Wing and began the long, narrow walk down the corridor. It could have been the hallway of any hotel. Patterned, plush carpeting, earth - tone colored walls that were brightly lit. Glancing out the windows in the lobby just outside the elevators, Mike saw an incredible view that included a few clouds below them, along with abundant sunshine. It was like looking out the window of a stationary jet plane.

Gabriel held a key over the scanner of a door near the end of the hallway, and pushed it open for Mike to enter. Mike froze in the entrance.

"Is there a problem?" Gabriel asked.

"This...is my place," Mike stammered, after a

moment of silence.

"I told you that's where we were going."

"Yeah, but I didn't think you meant *my place.*"

The walls were white covering the wainscoting. The floors a polished hardwood. Windows ran on three sides with the fourth side home to a fireplace. There was a staircase with a wooden railing and stairs covered with an oriental runner rug. A brown leather recliner couch and matching love seat sat in front of an extraordinarily large flat screen plasma television.

"How?"

"How what?"

"We were in a hotel corridor 17 floors up. You push open a door and I'm back in Connecticut?"

"You're not really in Connecticut. Not yet anyway. But we want you to be comfortable."

"What if I had lived in a dump?" Mike asked.

"Then maybe we would have upgraded it a bit," Gabriel laughed.

"So, how does this work?" Mike asked again.

He remained pretty skeptical, although the trick of recreating his house up in the sky, went a long way towards changing his mind. But he still couldn't remove the thought that he was dreaming. One of those dreams that seem like a dream, with just enough touches of reality to make you wonder. He began to pinch himself, wincing in the process.

"You're not dreaming."

How did he know what Mike was thinking? And that was exactly the thing someone would say in a dream to make you think it was real. He decided he wouldn't know the truth until he woke up, so he might as well go along with it.

"Ok. So how *exactly* does it work?" he asked for a third time.

"Pick any five days you like. Some people choose to relive days they loved. Others decide to revisit days they regretted and try to fix things. Most people use a combination of the two. But I have to warn you. Don't try to change the world, Mike. Because for every decision you make, there will be an entirely different set of consequences."

"What if I don't know specific dates?"

"Your computer can help you narrow that down," Gabriel answered. "It can access just about anything. But if you can't find the exact date, do the best you can. Describe the day, and that should be enough."

Mike went into the kitchen and looked in the refrigerator. A few slices of pizza, a jar of olives, a jug of water and a six-pack were the only contents. Just like on earth.

"Once I've picked the days, then what?" he asked as he popped open a beer. He motioned to Gabriel to see if he wanted one as well, but Gabriel shook his head.

"Write them on a piece of paper, put it in an envelope, and slide it under your door. You'll wake up tomorrow morning on the first day you chose."

"And after the 5th day, I come back here?" Mike asked.

"That all depends on what you decide to do with your days," Gabriel responded simply. "A piece of advice. Think carefully about it."

"My life wasn't all that exciting," Mike said dryly.

"You'll be surprised at how exciting your life will seem when you can only choose five days from it," Gabriel answered.

"Thanks. I guess. I suppose I'll see you eventually."

Gabriel nodded as he pulled the door shut behind him. "Let's hope later rather than sooner," Gabriel said to himself once he was safely in the hallway.

Mike had just sat down on the couch, when there was a knock on the door.

"Forget something Gab—" he said as he pulled open the door.

He stopped mid-sentence and froze even more rigidly than he had before when he saw a smiling, late teenage girl on the other side of it. It had been a long time, more than twenty years to be accurate, and time had a way of cruelly fading even some of his most cherished memories to the point where he began to wonder whether they had ever really happened at all, or were more the product of a vivid imagination that remembered things and people as he wanted to remember them. But almost immediately, emotions and feelings flooded into him that he hadn't felt in years, and his heart began to skip a beat to the same pattern it did anytime she had walked into a room.

"Oh my god," he gasped. "Kylie."

IV

˜A BLAST FROM THE PAST˜

*K*ylie Peters had been a bit of a tomboy growing up. She wasn't afraid of getting dirty, while doing all the things little boys did. She played in the mud, tried to melt ants with magnifying glasses, skateboarded, shot hoops, and even played tackle football until the boys got a little too rough and big. But Mike lost touch with her after middle school, when his parents sent him to private school. Even though they lived exactly 52 steps from each other—Mike had counted one time—their exchanges in high school had consisted of a wave from the porch or a yell of *"hey you"* from an open car window, until Kylie showed up at his school one morning with intentions of transferring. Until that moment, Mike had barely acknowledged she was a female, much less an attractive one.

With blonde curls that bounced every single time she took a step, blue-eyes as clear as crystal, a beautiful smile and a sing-songy voice that was befitting of a person that almost never seemed to be in a foul mood, she was the girl next door, literally, and figuratively. She was also beautiful, with long legs and an athletic body that on those rare occasions she decided to show it off, had the power to create traffic accidents and a number of sprained necks. When she re-entered Mike's life in January of his junior year, his world was changed forever.

"Expecting someone else?" she asked as she stood in the hallway of heaven, outside his house in the sky.

Mike was stunned. Speechless. He wouldn't have been more surprised if he had opened the door and been smashed across the head by his grandmother holding a two by four.

"Truthfully, I was expecting just about *anyone* else," he finally answered.

"Well, you are in heaven. Where did you think they sent me?"

"I guess I haven't really had time to think about it."

"I'm just teasing. I remember how confusing the first day was."

She let herself in and looked around. "Nice place."

She was wearing a fairly form-fitting, royal blue striped, button down with the top two buttons undone, a pair of khaki shorts with flip flops, that combined to show enough of her legs and rear end that Mike could not help but notice. She smiled when she saw him looking.

"It's ok. You can look. I don't mind."

"I wasn't looking."

"I saw your reflection off the picture," she winked.

Mike leaned to look at the picture to see if that was even possible.

"We go way back. It's fine," she laughed.

"How did you know I was here?" he asked, in a desperate effort to change the subject.

"They notified everyone you were close with, so we could help you feel more comfortable. But from what I understand, you're not going to be here that long."

"I'm not really sure how that works," he answered uncomfortably.

"You died a hero," she responded.

"I wouldn't exactly call me that."

"Do you want to get something to eat?" she asked. "The food's pretty good around here."

"Sure," he said distractedly. "I'm sorry, I can't get over how—"

"--young I look?" she finished his sentence for him. "You forever stay the age you were when you died. Unless you're old when you die, then you can choose."

"So you'll always be—"

"22 years younger than you? Yes."

"I'm not sure I like that," Mike said.

"Get over it, old man," she said playfully. "You don't have a choice. Besides, I only look young. Our souls are the same age. And it's really not how you look that's important. It's how you feel."

Mike felt old. And dead. It wasn't a good start to the reunion.

The Sports Page could have been a sports bar in any town U.S.A. A dozen flat screen televisions showed a variety of sporting events from baseball to horse racing to Texas Hold 'em Poker.

"I can't believe they're showing the World Series up here," Mike said. "And I can't believe the Cubs are actually winning it."

"They show everything you enjoyed down below," Kylie answered as she stuffed a beef and guacamole covered nacho chip into her mouth. Mike looked somewhat horrified.

"I don't remember you as having that big an appetite," he said.

"That's because when you knew me, I was an athlete who had to worry about gaining weight. I don't have to worry about lb's or cholesterol up here."

"My cholesterol was over 240," Mike said. "I probably would have been dead in a couple of years anyway."

"The only thing you have to worry about up here is how it tastes," she said with a smile. "So tell me," she continued, "Why'd you do it?"

Gabriel was smooth. When he didn't get the answers he wanted, he brought in the closer. He brought in the one person he knew Mike could never lie to. He brought in someone so sweet and so perfect, and yet someone, who had their own life taken away from them when they were only seventeen.

"It's kind of a long story," Mike said.

"I've got nothing but time," she answered.

V

~THE BEGINNING OF THE END~

*S*et high atop a grassy and tree covered hill in suburban Connecticut, Monroe High School more closely resembled a minimum security prison than a high school. The architecture was simple, the grounds clean, and there wasn't a single person in sight outdoors as the mid-November sun struggled in its quest to create some warmth.

Inside Mike Postman's freshmen Algebra class, the bell had just rung and several late arriving students shuffled to their seats, not showing the urgency they might have shown a different teacher. Mike was the popular teacher. Youngish, funny, good looking; they respected him, but also knew he wouldn't make a big issue about them being late as long as they didn't make a habit of it.

Mike began to read off his attendance list, looking up every couple of names to see if the voice answering *"here"* actually was the person in question. Under the glass on one corner of his desk was an article from a local newspaper about a friend of his who had been killed in 9/11.

"Mr. Hicks," Mike said.

"Here."

"Mr. Jones."

"Here."

"Ronan the Barbarian."

A tiny brunette girl in the front of the room smiled shyly and shook her head. Another girl answered for her. "Why do you always make fun of Kristin?"

"Because it's so easy, Miss Doyle."

"That's not very nice," the girl responded.

"I never claimed to be nice, Miss Doyle."

The door to the classroom opened and another girl attempted and failed to enter unnoticed.

"Ah, Miss Spazato. Nice of you to find time for us in your busy schedule. Thanks for dropping in today."

"No problem," the girl replied with a smile.

Two boys had been playing around in the back of the room the entire time. One knocked the other's book off his desk.

"As soon as Mr. Phillips and Mr. Mulligan are finished playing grab-ass in the back of the room, we can get started."

The class roared and the boys finally stopped; embarrassed by the attention. The room finally fell silent.

"Now..." Mike began, just as there was a soft knock at the door. A sorrowful looking girl entered, but didn't say anything. Lisa Wolper was sixteen going on thirty-five. She was harshly pretty, with too much makeup, too high heels, and too little clothing in general.

"Excuse me a second, will you?" he said to the

class. "I'll be right back. Check your homework answers with these sheets."

He tossed a couple of answer keys on his desk and followed the girl into the hallway, closing the door to the room behind them.

"So what's the word, Leese?" Mike asked.

She answered plainly, "I'm pregnant."

It was clear from the expression on his face that it wasn't the answer he was expecting. "Are you sure?"

"I wasn't sure this morning, but I just came back from Planned Parenthood."

Mike bit down on his lower lip, and fell against the wall for support.

"I need some advice," she said.

"I'm not sure I'm qualified to help you," Mike answered.

"Well, you can't give any worse advice than my brother did," she replied. "He told me to use a condom next time."

"That's not terrible advice," Mike shrugged, "although maybe a bit like closing the barn door after the horse has already gotten out."

"What about now? Tell me what I should do?" Lisa said, showing cracks of emotion for the first time.

"I can't do that. That's something for you, your family and the father to decide. Who is the father anyway?"

"Dan."

"The 22 year old?!" Mike exclaimed.

"Yeah."

"Have you told him?"

"Last night."

"And what was his reaction?"

"His reaction was to move to Colorado. He's leaving tonight."

"He does know that you're only sixteen, right?"

"Ummm..."

"Lisa," he said, trying to withhold a lecture.

"I meant to tell him. But now, there doesn't seem like there's much point."

"Well, I know this probably won't be all that comforting, but it sounds like you'll be better off without him," Mike said.

"You're right," Lisa answered, "That's not very comforting."

"Are you in love with the guy?"

"Of course not. I barely know him. But I need his money."

"He doesn't sound all that responsible. Besides, that's not a very good reason to stay with someone."

She knew he was right, but didn't want to admit it. Her eyes shifted away from him the way most embarrassed sixteen year olds tended to. "But I can't support a baby on my own. My mother's barely making it as a waitress."

"Then that's something to consider," Mike said.

"So, you don't think I should have the baby?" she asked.

"I didn't say that."

"So you think I should?"

"I didn't say that either," Mike answered.

"Then what should I do?" Lisa wailed.

"Unfortunately, I can't make that decision for you. But, what I can do, is help you sort out your options. In addition to the options you're already considering, you might want to look into putting the baby up for adoption."

"I don't think I could do that."

"It wouldn't be easy," Mike said. "None of the choices are. But you have to look at not only what's in your best interest, but also what would be in the best interest of the baby as well. Would you have the money to support it? You also have to consider what kind of job you'd be able to get without a high school or college education if you dropped out. And if you decided to come back, you'd have to consider who would be available to watch your baby and how much that would cost."

"I hadn't really thought of all that," Lisa said softly.

"How far along are you?" Mike asked.

"Three and a half months."

"So, you're due around mid-April?"

"Something like that," she answered.

"Theoretically, you could get incompletes in your classes, finish up during the summer and return in the fall if you wanted."

"I don't think I'm coming back, Mr. Postman."

"Why not?"

"School's just not for me. I want to be a hairdresser."

"School's not for anyone. But you need it in order to make something of your life. It teaches you to reason, and it teaches you discipline. I'd understand it a bit more if you didn't have the ability to do well."

"I don't know," Lisa wavered.

"You can always become a hairdresser later,"

Mike said. "But at least if you finish school, you'll have other options as well."

"I'll think about it," she said unconvincingly.

"Sounds like you've got a lot to think about," Mike said.

"Thanks for listening, Mr. Postman."

"I wish I could do more to help."

"You've done more than you think," she answered. "And you know something? If I do decide to keep the baby, I'm going to name him after you."

"What if it's a girl?" Mike asked.

"Then I'll name her Michelle," she said.

Mike smiled faintly. "Fair enough."

"Well, you should probably get back to your class," she said as she noticed a few paper airplanes in flight through the window on the door.

Mike nodded awkwardly as he turned the handle.

"And Mr. Postman?"

He turned back around. "Yeah, Leese?"

"Aren't you even going to say I told you so?"

"Why would I say that?"

"Because you were right about the guy."

"Maybe so," he began, "but I would have rather been wrong."

Thirty minutes later, the bell rang and students flooded into the hallway. Mike exited his classroom and was too preoccupied to even notice a pretty young teacher as he walked past her. Bridget O'Leary was a petite woman in her mid-twenties, with auburn hair and green eyes that were a brilliant shade of green rarely seen. She wasn't gorgeous, but was adorable in her own quiet, unassuming manner.

"Someone's got a lot on their mind," she said.

"Huh? What? Sorry," was Mike's disjointed response.

"I understand you made tenure," she continued. "Congratulations."

"They only did it to cover their ass," he answered, downplaying it. "They figured it was cheaper than a lawsuit."

"You don't really think that, do you?"

"I *know* that."

"What difference does it make anyway? You know you're an excellent teacher. At least now you've got some job security."

"Yeah. At a place where the kids don't give a damn. The funny thing is, these same kids who don't want to be here now, will be willing to give up just about anything ten years from now to be back here."

"We were the same way when we were their age. That's just human nature. Never appreciating what you have while you still have it."

"Maybe so," Mike said, softening somewhat, "but we had respect for our teachers. And maybe we didn't like the work, but we did it anyway because we knew it was going to provide us with any opportunities we might have later in life. These kids can't see past the end of their noses."

"Then it's up to you to help them do that," Bridget responded.

"How? By helping them get kicked out? Hell, I'm the solution to overcrowding in the schools. Want to get rid of a few kids? Have them come work with me."

"That's not true."

"Isn't it? It was for J.R. Ramirez and Rick Kennedy. And now Lisa Wolper. She'll probably withdraw. And what about Bill Dipoto? Looks like he's on his way out as well."

"The only reason Lisa Wolper has lasted this long is because of you. And what about Tim? I thought he was back on the baseball team?"

"He quit," Mike answered flatly.

"Well, you can't save everyone, Mike. No matter how badly you might want to."

"I'd be happy if I got through to *anyone*."

"And you have. Those kids are all better off for knowing you."

"You'd never know it. Even my boss at the talent agency said *'thank you'* once in a while."

"So, that's what this is about," Bridget said, the light bulb going off in her head. "You don't feel appreciated. Well, let me enlighten you. Just because these kids don't say thank you, doesn't mean they don't appreciate you. It only means they don't know how to say thank you."

Mike kicked at a crumpled piece of paper that lay on the ground. "That's not what this is about," he said unconvincingly. "I don't expect you to understand. I'm not sure I do myself."

"Giving of yourself without expecting anything in return," Bridget said. "That is the very essence of teaching. And also it's beauty."

"That's easy to say for someone who's leaving at the end of the semester."

"That's not fair. I'm getting married and moving."

"You're right. It's not fair. But I've got to go. I'll talk to you later," Mike said as he began to walk down the otherwise deserted corridor. He looked for some signs of life in the darkened classrooms, finding none, until a poster on the nurse's office door caught his eye. He approached it slowly, the words becoming clearer as he drew near.

"Every child needs to have at least one person who believes in them. You will never know how important your love and support can be to a struggling child. It could be the one thing that provides them with some measure of hope in the face of despair."

Mike bit down on his lip as he continued slowly toward the exit.

VI

~AND THE TRUTH SHALL SET YOU FREE~

*T*he restaurant remained crowded with older people, even as the time pushed on towards 9:00pm. There were no early bird specials in heaven. There was no need for them, as everyone had bountiful energy and no worries about their digestive tracts. People ate as if it was their last meal, gorging themselves, and yet they never felt overly full. Eating was no longer to maintain strength or health. It was simply for the taste of it. A pleasure like alcohol or sex.

"I thought people that died old could choose what age they want to be in heaven?" Mike asked. It was obviously bothering him.

"They can choose how others *see* them. It's kind of like a Facebook privacy setting. Different people can see different things."

Kylie shoveled the last spoonful of chocolate mousse into her mouth and swallowed it with a delightful smile as Mike looked on. She dropped her spoon to clank around the now empty glass dish and looked up.

"Sounds like you had a tough day," she said at last.

"It wasn't just that," Mike answered. "I'd had plenty of tough days. But usually, I would go home and go to sleep, and when I woke up, everything would be ok again. But on that day, I never made it home. I went straight to the beach, and that's where I ran into the little boy."

"I see," Kylie said.

"Like I told Gabriel. I didn't have a bad life. It was just—ordinary, and I guess I expected more. I'll be honest with you, Ky. If the opportunity hadn't presented itself, I never would have done it. But there's nothing I can do about that--" he stopped himself mid-sentence.

"Something wrong?" she asked.

"Those guys over there," Mike said, pointing to a group of men at the bar, who had the look of a group of golfers, "the one in the visor. He looks just like..."

"Tom?" she answered.

"Yeah. Tom. And the one next to him looks like a guy I grew up with who was killed in 9/11."

"That's because it is. He broke the course record yesterday. Shot a 65."

"And Tom looks so...healthy."

"That's because he is. Runs five miles every morning. Plays 36 holes every day."

"When we were kids, the doctors said with his heart condition, he probably wouldn't see 13. I used to run for him in baseball. He was the automatic quarterback in football. And the goalie in street hockey. Next thing you know he was 20. Then 25.

He was always a good golfer, but even that became a bit of a struggle towards the end. He was 36 when he died," Mike said. "Todd was in the north tower of the Trade Center when the planes hit. He was only 34."

"Why don't you go over and say hello?"

"I don't know," Mike answered awkwardly.

"Is it because you feel guilty?" she asked.

"Why would I feel guilty?" Mike asked defensively.

"Because both of them would give anything just so they could have one more day on earth, and you gave your opportunity away."

If anyone else had said that, Mike would have tossed a few expletives their way and walked out, but Kylie wasn't anyone. Besides, she was right.

"Go over," she urged. "I'll stop by later on."

Mike slowly made his way across the room, unsure of what he was going to say when he got there.

"Gentlemen," he said, tapping Tom on the shoulder.

"Hey, buddy," Tom answered, smiling brightly. He didn't seem the least bit surprised to see him. "We heard you were here."

"How are you doing?" Mike asked. "You both look great."

"I feel great. Todd shot a 65 yesterday."

"I heard. You always were a helluva golfer for a soccer player."

"How's your golf game?" Todd asked.

"Not great. I got frustrated playing righty, so I started playing lefty. Now, I alternate shots depending on how I feel."

"Only you would do something like that," Tom laughed. "I hear you're going back."

He said it so matter-of-factly, as if they were talking about a vacation he was going on.

"Yeah," Mike answered sheepishly. "I kind of feel like I owe you guys an apology for that."

"Why on earth would you say that?"

"I don't know. I just do."

"Look, Mike, we could lie to make you feel better, but the truth is this. I'm jealous as hell. I'd give anything to have even one more day with my wife and son. I didn't think it was possible to miss people as much as I miss them," Todd lamented.

"And I feel great, better than I ever felt on earth, but it's not the same," Tom added. "I never got to feel the wind whipping through my hair as I ran when I was nine. I never got to score the winning touchdown in a high school football game. And I never got to feel what it was like to fall in love, because I never let anyone get close enough. I knew with my health, it was only a matter of time, and I didn't want to put anyone through that. So, yeah, I'm jealous as hell too, but I'm happy for you. Just promise me one thing."

"Anything."

"Make the most of it this time. And then, call us when you get back and we can go break some windows on the golf course. The conditions are always perfect up here."

Then he smiled a warm smile, which only made Mike feel all the worse.

* * *

Mike must have taken twenty-five laps around the fountain pool in the courtyard before returning to his room. He was having a difficult time thinking clearly since seeing his old friends. Guilt had a way of wearing one down. He found Kylie waiting for him when he finally arrived.

"How were Tom and Todd?" she asked.

"A lot nicer than I would have been," Mike responded.

"What did they say?"

"To make the most of it this time."

He clearly didn't want to talk much about it. Doing so, only made him feel more guilty than he already did.

"You know, Mike," she began, "I can understand just about everything you said earlier, except for one thing."

"What's that?"

"When you said you thought your life was ordinary," she answered. "You lived through some of the greatest and most horrific events in history. Some of them you witnessed from afar. Others, up close. You saw the best and the worst in people. There are a lot of words I would use to describe your life--but *ordinary* isn't one of them."

She ran her hand through his hair, leaned in, and kissed him on the cheek. "It was great seeing you again," she said. "I'm going to miss you all over."

"I'll see you tomorrow," Mike said with conviction. She smiled, even though she wasn't sure exactly what he meant by that.

Mike sat down at his computer for hours that night, occasionally printing something out that he would study as if he was memorizing for a test. He looked back at the events of his life, at least the best he could recall them.

Out of the corner of his eye, he saw a bound, covered book along with a single DVD lying on one corner of the coffee table. It definitely wasn't there before. The book contained photos, letters and newspaper articles from his life. A note scribbled on the cover of the DVD read, *"Thought this might help. G"*

He inserted it into the player and leaned back onto his favorite couch, the way he had done hundreds of times before, as the DVD began to play.

VII

~LEESE~

Mike's resume looked like it had been made up by a third grader. Not in the way it was written. But because it contained so many different previous jobs that it seemed like somebody's son was trying to impress his friends with all of the things his father had done. Notre Dame undergrad. Syracuse's Newhouse School of Communications for grad school. A cameraman for the evening news. A videotape editor for a production company. A producer for a kid's game show on PBS. Further conversation revealed he had also been a baggage handler for an airline and a clerk in the shipping department of a plastic factory.

Normally, we wouldn't have even considered hiring him at Entertainers and Athletes Agency—a place where focus, stability and relationships were everything. But there was just something about him that made us feel as though we'd be missing out if we didn't hire him.

In a business where actors complained if they didn't have a trailer large enough to fit a full-sized pool inside it, Mike was a breath of fresh air. He would fire rubber bands at his co-workers while they were in the middle of phone conversations, and set hidden alarm clocks to simultaneously go off in what sounded like a bad rendition of Beethoven's 5th Symphony. People were drawn to him. Whenever Adam Sandler or Tom Cruise entered the building, most were too nervous to even spit out a greeting, but not Mike. He would talk to anyone at anytime—even when I didn't want him to.

As an assistant agent, sometimes referred to as a junior agent, Mike had to be able to perform several tasks at once. It was not unusual for him to be talking on the phone, typing a contract, signing for a package and reading notes on a script for a client all at once. Perhaps most important as a junior agent was a need to lie to nearly everyone about everything in order to make me look better and keep things moving along. He was the master at that. Clients loved him, and most importantly, they trusted him. And maybe that took its toll on him.

Because just as suddenly as he had arrived, Mike was gone. I helped him line up a job in New York City with a television news show, but the show got cancelled just before he left. He could have stayed with me and eventually been promoted to a job that paid him a fortune. He decided to move closer to his family and became a teacher. Go figure. Most people would have chosen money. But Mike wasn't built that way.

All I know is that he could have been one of the great power brokers in all of Hollywood. The guy could have sold ice to the Eskimos. Convincing a studio to hire one of our actors would have been easy for him in comparison.

"It's harder to learn to love a job where you make money," he explained to me one day, "then it is trying to make money at a job you love."

To be completely honest, I never really understood what he meant by that. It was like he was speaking in a foreign language or something.

* * *

I worked with Mike Postman at Monroe High School for seven years, which was long enough to know that the popular teachers are usually the ones who taught the classes the students actually enjoyed, like gym, art or music. Mike was the only popular teacher I ever knew who taught Math.

I shared the classroom next to his, and it used to drive me crazy, because I would hear constant screaming and shouting to the point where I thought maybe he had stepped out of the room for a minute. So I'd go next door and look in the window, and sure enough, he'd be there, right in the middle of one of his crazy invented games like "Mathketball" or "Math 'o Fortune". The students would be running around, shouting, throwing paper towards the trashcan that he was holding up, enjoying themselves. Most of all, they would be learning.

His students on average scored almost 10 points higher on the department midterms and finals than students in other classes did, mostly because he wouldn't accept anything less than their best. Sadly, I don't think Mike ever realized the influence he had on them. Instead of acknowledging the 200 students he helped each year, he would be focused on the three or four he hadn't been able to reach. I guess *that's what made him so good at what he did.*

As someone who struggled in Math her entire life, I found it that much more amazing that he was able to generate interest in it. Students who normally didn't do a stitch of work in other classes, worked in Mike's. Students who were normally disruptive, behaved in his classes. I asked him one day why that was, and I'll never forget his answer. He told me students will act in whatever manner we expect them to. If you expect them to misbehave, they will. But if you expect them to work, they will. Most importantly, if you expect them to respect you, you have to respect them first.

Of course, I'm saddened that he won't be around any longer talk to, joke with, or make fun of what I was wearing. But I think I'm most saddened by the fact that he died without ever realizing how important he was to the school and to those of us that knew him.

* * *

I've been a "D" student pretty much all my life, starting back in the first grade when I couldn't color between the lines. But I got "B's" in Mr. Postman's Algebra class and not because he was an easy teacher. It was because he wouldn't accept anything less from me. He would follow me down the corridor and hand me sample problems to work on. He would stop into my study hall to make sure I had done my homework. And he would stay after school to help me whenever I asked, and sometimes, even when I didn't.

He was the first teacher I ever had who got me to believe in myself. If I go on to graduate, it will be because of him, and in some respects, for him. He was a father figure or big brother as he would have preferred, for those of us who didn't have one.

But more than anything, he was a friend. He listened to endless stories and problems of mine, never once looking down or judging me for my stupid decisions, and believe me when I tell you there have been plenty of them.

I will be sad not having him around anymore, but I think I'll feel even sadder for those who never even had the opportunity to know him at all.

* * *

For a reason he couldn't quite pinpoint if you asked him, Lisa's eulogy touched Mike more than any of the others. Maybe it was the simple sincerity of it. Maybe it was because she was able in a few short sentences explain to him what he never believed was true. Whatever the reason, after hearing her speak, Mike suddenly knew what he needed to do.

He flipped through the book Gabriel had left him and the memories came flooding back to him so thick that he needed both arms to wave them away from his face. He was reminded of the last time he saw his grandparents. The first time he saw his nephew. His first kiss. Scoring the winning goal in the homecoming soccer game. Gabriel was right. There were so many days. But in the end, five of them, stood out more than any of the others.

He used his computer to help find their actual dates, scribbled them down on a sheet of paper which he put into an envelope, and slid it underneath his door, just as Gabriel had said.

He then tossed and turned in his bed while the minutes and hours continued to change, occasionally getting up to pace around the room. Eventually, tiredness overcame him and he drifted off to sleep.

VIII

~BEST FRIENDS FOREVER~

Mike fell in love with Kylie Peters the moment he met her. He just didn't know it at the time because he was only six. She arrived on the doorstep of the Postman household as they prepared to leave for a Syracuse game.

"I'm Kylie Peters," she announced to Mr. Postman. "We just moved in next door and I heard you have two kids. Do you think either of them would like to come out and play?"

"We do, in fact, have two kids. Jacklyn is probably a few years older than you, and Mike, well, he's probably about your age. How old are you?"

"I'm six."

"Then he's exactly your age. And I'm sure they'd love to play with you if we weren't getting ready to leave for a football game."

"I like football," she said. "Although I'd rather play it than watch it."

"Is that so?" Mr. Postman chuckled.

Taking in the exchange from the top of the staircase was Mike, and that's exactly where he would have remained if his father hadn't ushered him down.

"Mike! Get your butt down here and meet our new neighbor!"

He trudged down the steps and looked questioningly at the girl who would soon become his new best friend.

"Hi. I'm Mike. I live here."

"I know that. I'm visiting *you* remember? I'm Kylie."

She held out her hand unflinchingly. Mike shook it tentatively as Mr. Postman chuckled to himself.

"Maybe we can play football sometime," she added.

"Maybe," he answered.

"Looks like you've got another player for your games," Mr. Postman said as they both watched her bounce across the lawn to her house.

"But she's a girl," Mike grimaced.

"She's probably tougher than you."

Mike still wasn't sure what to make of her, and yet, years later if you were to ask him the two clearest memories from his childhood, one would be the day the United States hockey team beat the Russians; the other would be meeting Kylie Peters for the first time.

FEBRUARY 22, 1980

DAY 1

IX

~THE SHOCK HEARD ROUND
THE WORLD~

Mike eyes grew wide when he realized the reflection looking back at him in the bathroom mirror was fourteen years old again. He forcefully rubbed the sleep from his eyes to make certain they weren't playing tricks on him, but indeed found that a few hours of beauty rest had managed to erase nearly 30 years of wrinkles and almost 40 pounds. He had the body of a 14 year old again. Nothing ached. He felt light on his feet. And he was starving for some Captain Crunch.

His mind, on the other hand, was a bit of a jumbled mess. He remembered things from all 40+ years, but his emotions were that of an excited teenager. He wanted to make one of his favorite days last as long as possible so instead of climbing back under the covers as he normally would have, he decided to stay up.

He tore a sheet of paper out of a notebook, making certain that there were no fringes on the sheet. He hated them as a teacher because the papers would all stick together, and it traced back to when he was a kid. He had what would eventually be diagnosed some years later as a mild case of Obsessive Compulsive Disorder.

Mike scribbled down in handwriting that was actually far neater than it would be later in life, times, names and what appeared to be locations, none of which made much sense, then folded the paper up.

"Where can I put it that I won't end up throwing it out?" he said to himself before his eyes settled on a shoebox of baseball cards in his closet. He stuffed the paper in the middle of the box and went downstairs.

"Thanks for making breakfast this morning," Mr. Postman said as he kissed his wife.

"Don't thank me. Thank your son," was her response.

"Good one," Mr. Postman laughed. "You can't make breakfast in your sleep, and Mikey hasn't been up before eight o'clock on a weekend or a vacation day his entire life."

Mr. Postman's claim to fame was that he made breakfast every morning. Not that it was a tremendous feat, mind you. It consisted of setting the table, putting out some cereal boxes and squeezing the orange juice. It wasn't as if he was whipping up pancakes and creating deep-dish omelets. But for a man who once had to call his son in college when his wife was out of town, just to figure out how to turn on the oven, it was an accomplishment of epic proportions.

Mike entered the kitchen almost as if on cue. "Got a football game to play today," he said.

"Make sure you invite Kylie," his mother said.

"But she's a girl," Mike whined.

"She's tougher than you," his father chided.

Mike grew up in a children-laden, middle to upper middle class neighborhood in suburban Connecticut. It was the perfect street to live on. A long cul-de-sac with 12 homes, 10 of which had kids between the ages of 12 to 17. There were the twins. The Chang brothers. Kylie and her brother. And there was David. As the oldest and best athlete, David was the unofficial leader who organized the games that ran the length of three backyards and lasted more than five hours. Which sport they played depended on the number of people who were available and allowed to play. Back in the 80's kids actually asked their parents for permission to play. Nowadays, parents would have to beg them to go outside and get some fresh air, instead of staying glued to the couch playing Wii or Xbox. The other variable was the weather. February in Connecticut could be cold and clear, cold with two feet of snow on the ground, rainy and damp, or spring-like with temperatures in the 60's. Occasionally, it was all of the above on the same day. Poor conditions would eliminate soccer, baseball and basketball as options. But football, could be played in any weather.

Since it was a vacation week, everyone was around. David put the twins and the Changs on one team, and Kylie, her brother Jeff, and Mike on the other team with him. Their ever-increasing age had forced the evolution of the game to go from tackle to two-hand touch, in part to prevent injuries, but also because they were at that age where they didn't want to touch Kylie in a place where they shouldn't, even if it was by accident. But with a foot of powdery snow on the ground and temperatures in the 20's, feeling much of anything was unlikely.

"This is it," David announced after they had been playing for about three and a half hours. "Next score wins."

"What *is* the score?" one of the Changs asked.

"84-80," Mike answered. Numbers were his thing.

"84-80," David repeated.

"How do you have 84?!" one of the twins demanded.

"We converted three two-point conversions. A pass from me to Jeff. Mike on an end around. And me on a quarterback sneak. But it doesn't matter anyway. If you score, you win 86-84. If we score, we win 90-80 and set a new Acreage Farm scoring record!"

No one was gong to argue with David, because they knew above all else, he valued honesty. Mike was also convinced that David could have been an offensive coordinator for any NFL team. He knew all the tricks. The Hitch and Pitch. Hook and ladder. Statue of Liberty. Double reverse. Halfback option. And the always popular, "run to the tree stump, then streak across the middle of the field while the other receiver makes a bee-line for the oak tree".

"Here's the play," David said. "Mike and Jeff. You guys line up wide right. Kylie. You line up on the left. Jeff, you're going to run a ten yard buttonhook pattern. As soon as I get it to you, pitch it back to Mike, who's going to be right on your ass. Mike, then look immediately across the field for

Kylie, who should be wide open. But Kylie, make sure you're even or behind Mike, so it counts as a lateral."

She nodded.

"Ready. On 3. Break!"

One of the Changs lined up to rush the passer. The other picked up Kylie, but shaded toward where Mike and Jeff were lined up, while the twins covered them. The ball was snapped on the third count and the older Chang counted to 5 Mississippi before rushing. Jeff ran his pattern, but slipped in the snow when he turned for the ball. David, facing a fierce pass rush, had already released it. The pass hit Jeff in the head and bounded straight into the air. The twins collided as they went for the ball and Mike ended up tapping it to himself. As the younger Chang bore down on him, he looked across the field and heaved a glove addled pass towards Kylie. She caught it and raced untouched into the endzone. Chaos ensued. Kylie jumped straight into Mike's arms, while David and Jeff dog piled on. The other team complained that it was an illegal forward pass, even though they all knew that it wasn't. One of the twins kicked the snow and it flew directly into his brother's face, who then shoulder slammed him to the ground in frustration.

"Hey, what time is it?!" Mike shouted as he helped Kylie up, her blue eyes peering out from beneath her knit scuffo admiringly.

"4:55," David answered.

"The hockey team is playing Russia in five minutes!"

"Yeah, but they're not going to show it until eight

o'clock tonight."

"I've got a pretty good feeling that one of the cable channels might just show it live," Mike said knowingly.

The eight of them proceeded to crowd around the 16 inch Sony color television with the round channel dial and the push button cable box in the Postmans' living room, since they were the only family in the neighborhood to have cable at the time. Mike punched about 10 channels before they finally found the game.

"There it is!" one of the twins shouted.

Most television network affiliates planned to run a tape delay of the game later that night, partly because they thought they would get better ratings during prime time, but also because no one figured it would be much of a game. Two weeks prior to the Olympics, the United States Hockey team had been embarrassed by the Soviet Union 10-3 at Madison Square Garden in New York. There was no reason to believe it would be much different this time— especially after Russia scored first. But the crowd in Lake Placid came to life when the USA tied the game a few minutes later, only to be quieted when Russia took the lead back.

In the final seconds of the first period, however, the Russian goalie made an error that not only helped the USA tie the game once again, but injected life into an arena and a country. By this time, everyone else in the neighborhood was also now in the Postman living room. Most of them weren't even hockey fans. But this was more than a hockey game. This was about national pride. This was us against them. It was the Cold War. And Afganistan. And boycotted Olympics. Our college kids against professionals. In fact, it was one of the last times the US used amateurs to compete in the Olympics.

Russia took command in the 2nd period but had only a one goal lead to show for their efforts. The chants of "U-S-A U-S-A" only grew louder with each passing moment, both in the arena, and in Mike Postman's living room. When the US tied the game early in the 3rd period, everyone jumped to their feet in celebration, and when they took the lead a minute later, they hugged each other in disbelief.

Ten minutes still remained, but there wasn't a soul anywhere in the country who was sitting down. Team USA's goalie, a young kid from Boston named Jim Craig, who had only come out for the team because it had been a dream of his mother before she died, put the team, and unknowingly, the country, on his back. In those last ten minutes, he turned away every shot, every deflection, every cross, every rebound. It was the stuff legends were made of, with every save being closely followed by "Ohhh!", "Oooo!" or "Wow!".

And when Al Michaels made the legendary call of "Do you believe in miracles?! YES!" the arena in Lake Placid and homes throughout the country erupted.

Forty-two people ended up in a heap in the middle of the room. Eventually, Mike freed himself from the pile and raced outside, in time to hear a chorus of honking horns, screaming, cheering, chanting and the national anthem being played out of distant windows from neighboring streets.

It was that way the rest of the day. Everywhere they went, flags were being flown off of car antennas. People were celebrating in the streets. For one day at least, the country was in complete harmony. Helping each other. Smiling at each other. Hugging each other. Most sporting events affected only a town, city or a school. This one had unified an entire country. And although no one knew it at the time, it was unlikely such an event would ever occur again.

Mike couldn't sleep that night, having just re-experienced a moment of his life that went pretty much unparalleled. He, and so many others like him, had told the story so many times over the years, that they sometimes wondered if they had exaggerated its greatness or people's reactions to it, but as Mike saw it unfold before his very eyes once again, he realized if anything, he had understated it. He planned to stay awake that night for as long as his eyelids would permit.

"What are you still doing up?" his mother asked as she stuck her head in the room.

"I'm not tired," was his response.

"Could have fooled me. You're going to need toothpicks to keep your eyes open soon."

"I don't want to go to sleep," he answered.

"Why not?" his mother asked.

"Because I don't want this day to end. It's my favorite day."

"You're still pretty young," his mother assured him, "I'm sure your best days are still to come."

"You'd be surprised," Mike said dryly.

"Try and get some sleep," she said as she kissed him on the forehead. "I'll see you in the morning."

"Yeah.   Some morning three years from now," Mike answered once she had left the room.

X

~HE WHO HESITATES~

Mike and Kylie quickly became best friends forever before there was even the *term* best friends forever. They played football together. And baseball. And soccer. And basketball. On rainy days they played board games and watched movies. They were inseparable. When she would stretch her legs out over his lap while watching television, he didn't think twice about it. She was one of the guys. And yet, everyone else could see there was something more. But most boys needed to be hit over the head with a two by four in order to understand how a girl felt. A brick wouldn't have done the job for Mike.

When she would give him a present at Christmas—usually something thoughtful like a jersey of his favorite player, or a game that he loved—he would fumble around awkwardly for a card his mother bought for him that he had barely signed. When they hit high school and she would hint that she wanted to be asked to his prom, Mike had one of his goofier friends ask her. She wasn't sure whether that was because he figured she'd be safe with the kid, because he didn't view the kid as a threat, or simply because he thought she was goofy too. She spent many a night pouring over his every move, motive and decision, the way all teenage girls do.

And that's pretty much how their relationship went—until the day she entered his high school for the first time. Maybe it was because he hadn't seen her as much in recent years. Maybe it was because his friends were fawning all over her. Maybe he was growing up after years of suffering from Peter Pan syndrome. But the day he laid his eyes on her in the courtyard during English class, would change his life forever.

He found himself inexplicably drawn to her. Her eyes that had always been "blue", were now crystal. Her hair, which had always been "curly", had waves that bounced every time she took a step. And her body that he had tackled a hundred times on the football field, was suddenly something that he couldn't bring himself to touch if she held up a billboard with directions on it. And yet, he managed to keep those feelings well beneath the surface. She didn't have a clue as to how he felt. Meanwhile, she looked at him the way she always did—the way she always had—as if the world began and ended at his very feet.

He drove her home after school that first day, loud music masking the awkwardness that had never been in the same room with the two of them before. But it wasn't a bad awkwardness. It was an awkwardness that was a precursor to something wonderful, except that sometimes, life, gets in the way. As he walked Kylie to her front steps with every intention of kissing her for the first time with a kiss that wasn't a peck on the cheek, he hesitated ever so briefly, but long enough for his friends to arrive to take him to a concert. She had to settle for a handshake.

And when he was awakened the following morning to the newscaster on his radio alarm announcing that Kylie Peters and her brother had been killed in a car accident the previous evening, two things never happened after that. Mike never allowed himself to get close to anyone. And he never used a radio alarm again.

AUGUST 27, 1983

DAY 2

XI

~THE GREAT GATSBY~

The relationship of children and their parents is a complicated one. When they are babies, they rely on their parents for everything. When they become toddlers, they idolize them. When they become teenagers, they still idolize them; they just don't want anyone to know it. By the time they hit their late teens, they think they have all the answers, until something goes horribly wrong and they need their parents to pick up the pieces. In August of 1983, Mike Postman was in full late teen mode.

His day usually consisted of his radio alarm going off at 6:30am, at which point he would feel around with his hand until he found the snooze button. Ten minutes later, it would go off again. This time he would hit the button with cat-like reflexes. The process would repeat itself two more times before his mother would enter, flip on every light in the room, rip open the curtains, and exit, making as much noise as possible during her brief visit. Once Mike realized he wouldn't be able to turn off the lights or close the curtains without actually leaving the comfy confines of his bed, then and only then, would he surrender to a new day.

Clad in a shirt, tie, khakis, and sneakers, Mike

walked through the kitchen in a hurry. He was seventeen now, with the attitude and demeanor to match.

"See you later, mom," he said.

"Aren't you going to eat something?" his mother asked, knowing full well the answer she was about to receive. Mothers of teenagers knew when they were fighting uphill and chose their battles very carefully.

"No time today," was the response.

"No time *any* day," Mrs. Postman answered.

"I'm a busy guy, mother."

"Well, busy guy, you better make time to be nice to Kylie today. Remember, this is her first day in a new school."

"Why did she transfer halfway through high school anyway?"

"Because she thought it would help her get into a better college. They didn't offer as many A.P. courses at her school."

"A.P. Schmapey," Mike said.

"It's nice to see that at least someone is concerned with their future."

"Whatever," Mike said with a shrug.

"Not whatever. Make sure you're nice to her," his mother warned.

"I'm always nice, mother."

"By *'nice'* I don't mean just saying *'hello'*. I know how you and your friends are."

"Don't worry. I'm sure by the end of the day we'll be tearing each others clothes off," Mike answered glibly.

"Don't get smart with me."

"I can't help it," he said with a smile. "I am

smart."

He reached into the open *Wheaties* box on the table and grabbed a handful of cereal.

"Breakfast of champions," he said as he kissed his mother goodbye.

Ten minutes later, he turned into a winding entrance that was surrounded by a creek on one side, and trees on both. The school building itself was made of old brick with ivy-covered walls and acres of open space that at one time had been nothing but forest. The parking lot was a virtual showroom of high-end automobiles and Mike nestled his mother's Pontiac Fiero in between a Porsche and a restored, 1967 Mustang convertible.

Mike's family, although comfortable, were definitely on the lower end of the economic spectrum at this school.

The bell sounded as Mike casually strolled down the corridor. Students began to pour into the hallway, and he poked his head into one of the open doorways.

"I'm here, Mr. Amblin," he said.

The teacher was fortyish, but still living in the 60's, with long red hair and sideburns to match. He followed Mike into the hallway.

"Mr. Postman, do you think that just once you could make it to homeroom on time?" he said.

"I'm sure that I could," Mike answered simply as he continued on his way.

"You think you've got all the answers, don't you Postman?!" Amblin yelled after him.

"I don't know how to tell you this, Mr. Amblin," Mike said as he turned back around, "but someone gave me the questions beforehand."

"Nice touch. Come in late. Then piss him off," Mike's friend, Jimmy said as he walked up.

"It's a dirty job, but someone has to do it," Mike answered.

"Well, you should have gotten to homeroom this morning for another reason altogether. The new girl is H-O-T."

"You mean, Kylie?" Mike asked incredulously.

"You *know* her?!" Jimmy asked.

"So do you, you idiot. It's the same girl who used to play football with us. And soccer. And basketball..."

"The tomboy?"

"That's the one."

"Well, she doesn't look like a tomboy anymore," Jimmy assured him, giving him something to think about as they headed to class.

Mike arrived at his English classroom and read the note on the board. *Junior English will meet outside in the courtyard.*

"Shit," Mike grumbled, as he ran for the stairwell.

Class was already underway by the time he arrived. Mr. Karmen was a book smart man also caught somewhere between the 60's and the 70's with wavy, unkempt greyish-black hair and a fu man chu style mustache. He wore a tie with a short-sleeved button down shirt, pants that were frayed at the bottom, and loose fitting brown sandals that exposed his overly hairy feet and jagged toenails.

"Sorry I'm late," Mike said as he sat down.

"—and so we beat on, boats against the current, borne back ceaselessly into the past," Karmen read.

"Mr. Postman, what do you think 'borne back ceaselessly into the past means'?"

"Oh, I don't know. Maybe being born backwards or something. Like a C section," Mike answered.

Karmen shook his head with equal parts disgust and hurt.

"Sorry. I haven't gotten that far yet," Mike offered in a conciliatory tone.

"Would that were true, Mr. Postman. But I doubt very seriously you have even opened the book at all," Karmen said.

"C'mon now, Mr. Karmen. I like a good book as much as the next guy."

Several students in the class tried unsuccessfully to stifle laughter. Karmen wasn't amused.

"That's exactly what I'm talking about," Karmen said, his voice rising. "You have no appreciation for literature!"

And with an amazed class looking on, Karmen clutched the book tightly to his chest, and stormed off, fighting back tears on his way.

"He's a little tightly wound, don't ya think?" one of the boys said to Mike.

"Ya think?" was Mike's reply.

"That's just great, Mike," an irritated girl responded. "What are we going to do now?"

"We're going to kick back and relax. Class is over," Mike said. "You're welcome."

"Must be nice to have all the answers," the girl continued.

"Valerie, it doesn't suck."

"Well, unlike you, some of us are actually here to

learn, and you're certainly not setting a very good example for our new student."

"It's not my fault Karmen's a loose wheel," Mike explained, "And aren't you going to introduce me to our new student?"

"And subject her to your obnoxiousness? Not a chance."

"That's ok. She's already been subjected to it," Mike said. "How are you, Kylie?"

"I'm good, Mike," she answered with a smile. "You?"

"Never better. So has Valerie done a good job of showing you around?"

"I've already introduced her to all the teachers, shown her the computer lab and the library, thank you very much," Valerie exclaimed proudly.

"For cryin out loud. You can't give a general admission tour to a VIP. C'mon, Kye. I'll show you the real school."

"But she's supposed to be with me," Valerie said, offended. "There's a reason they never let you show around new students."

"Yeah, they're afraid they might actually enjoy themselves."

Mike put his arm around Kylie and walked her back into the building. "First stop. The front desk."

"The front desk?"

"Trust me," Mike said with a wink as a girl walked past them. "What up, 'ho?" he said to her.

"Same shit, different day," the girl responded.

"I've got another newbie here," Mike said. "You guys should get to know each other."

"I'm late to class, but I'll find you guys later on,"

she answered.

"I'm not sure which is more offensive," Kylie said. "The fact that you called her a *'ho*, or the fact that she answered."

"It's a term of endearment. Blaire's new too. Makes her feel like one of the guys."

"Yes, I'm sure she loves it," Kylie laughed.

The woman behind the desk was an amiable older woman who was fast at work behind a paper-covered desk. She looked up with a smile as soon as she saw Mike.

"Kye. I want you to meet Mrs. Guenther. I don't care what anyone tells you. She runs the school," Mike said, before adding almost as an afterthought, "She's also the one in charge of late passes."

"And Mike would know," she responded.

"Did I mention she's also the sweetest, most wonderful person you'll ever meet?"

"Missed homeroom again this morning?" she said wryly.

"Mrs. Guenther, I'm insulted!" Mike said. "But yeah. Amblin's on the war path."

She scribbled on a piece of paper and tore it off. "You're going to get me fired one of these days," she said as she handed it to him.

"Hang in there. Only two more years until I graduate."

"I'd keep an eye on him if I were you," she said to Kylie, "He'd try to talk the stripes off a tiger."

Mike waved the pass at her. "Thank you. Same time tomorrow?"

Mrs. Guenther shook her head as she went back

to work.

"There's one other person you need to meet," Mike said to Kylie. "She's the only other person who can get you out of that Latin test you didn't have time to study for."

Mike knocked on the door of the nurse's office. A woman opened the door while still seated in her chair. She was on the phone, but waved them in. Mrs. Morris wore the typical sterile nurse's outfit. Navy slacks. Functional--which was another word to describe comfortable and ugly--white shoes. White button down shirt. An open buttoned down navy sweater.

"Hello, Mike," she said once she hung up the phone.

"Hi Mrs. M. I want you to meet a good friend of mine. This is Kylie Peters. Kye, this is Mrs. Morris. Kylie's a new student here."

"Nice to meet you, Kylie."

"Nice to meet you," Kylie said.

"So, Mike, how's that congestion of yours? Breathing any easier?"

"The decongestant you gave me worked like a charm. Thanks."

Kylie waited until they were out of earshot. "Latin test?"

"US History," Mike answered. "Tell me something. What are you doing tonight?"

"Going to visit my cousins in Watertown."

"Can you go up there tomorrow morning?" Mike asked.

"I'd have to ask my brother. He and I are driving up together. Why?"

"I've got an extra ticket to *The Police* tonight at Shea Stadium. *REM* and *Joan Jett* are opening for them. It's the hottest ticket around."

"How'd you end up with an extra ticket?"

"One of my sister's friends was supposed to go, but she's grounded. Tim's going. My sister. And you, if you can and want to."

"I'll call Jeff," she said. "It sounds like fun. I love *The Police*."

They all rode down together in Tim's family truckster—a 1977 Pontiac station wagon. Mike had forgotten how different the times were back then. The drinking age was 19 in New York State, with a grandfather clause for anyone who had turned 18 before they raised the age. And it wasn't a strict 19 either. If you had a library card or a piece of notebook paper with your picture stapled onto it, you could buy beer. Open alcohol containers, although not exactly encouraged, were not that frowned upon either.

Mike had gone on a road trip with Jimmy and Tim one time. They took turns driving, as the other two shot-gunned beers in the back. While stuck in traffic by a tollbooth on the New Jersey Turnpike, Jimmy vomited down the outside of the car as Mike pushed his head out the window. Onlookers were not impressed. But they didn't get arrested either.

This trip was a little less toxic. A few friendly beers were had to loosen the mood and to encourage dancing when they arrived at the concert, but nothing too crazy. They parked underneath a highway overpass about a quarter of a mile from the stadium and had a few more drinks before making the walk to the show.

Their seats were among the more than 10,000 people on the floor, about twenty-five rows back from the stage. In 1983, The Police were easily the most popular rock band in the world. The Synchronicity tour played to sold out stadiums throughout the globe. In fact, more than 67,000 people attended the Shea Stadium concert, or 12,000 more than were at *The Beatles* famous concert at Shea nineteen years earlier, almost to the day.

After opening with "Synchronicity I and II", they played all the favorites from "Roxanne" to "Message in a Bottle". People danced in the aisles and stood on chairs, which made viewing an impossibility at times.

Somewhat hidden, two rows up and about ten chairs over, a girl was eyeing Mike, but trying to make it look as though she wasn't. He noticed on the third go round.

"Excuse me a second," Mike said to Kylie as he made his way over to the girl.

"Jordo, what's a little girl like you doing in a place like this?" Mike asked.

"I'm not little," she answered defensively. "I'm 15."

"Who's this guy?" Mike asked, looking the boy over suspiciously.

The boy was her age, tall, thin and awkward, with braces, acne; the whole bit. He looked as if he wanted to crawl under the seats.

"This is Jeremy," Jordan answered, shaking her head for the interrogation she knew that would follow.

"When did you get out of jail, Jeremy?" Mike asked.

Jeremy looked as though he would be far more at home in a computer lab. He just smiled awkwardly at Mike's attempt at a joke.

"You know, Jord, you really need to stop scoping out the prison yards for dates. And I don't think you ran this one by me either. Your brother told me to keep an eye on you."

"He's met Jeremy and likes him," she said.

"All right then. But I'll be watching you J Dawg," Mike said, motioning with two fingers toward his eyes. "And Jordo, can I talk to you a second?"

"Sure. What's up?"

They walked into the aisle. It was still very loud. He had to shout above the music.

"How's your dad doing?" he asked.

"Seems to be a little better," she answered skeptically. "We're hoping to have him home in a few weeks."

She found it a strange time to be checking in on her family.

"Look, I don't know how to say this, so I'm just going to say it," Mike began.

"Say what?"

"Three days after your dad gets released from the hospital, he's going to seem like he's better, outwardly anyway. But he won't be. You need to have someone with him at all times making sure he stays on his meds."

"I don't understand."

"I know you don't. Just make sure he knows how much he means to your entire family. People usually forget about that fact."

"Why are you telling me this?!"

"Jord, he's going to try and kill himself. Don't ask me how I know. I just do. I can't explain it to you and you wouldn't believe me even if I could. But know that I would give anything for you to not have to go through the pain of losing him."

"Have you been drinking?" she asked skeptically.

"A little. But that has nothing to do with this. Hopefully everything will be ok. I had a favorite uncle who battled depression. We just didn't know what to look for until it was too late."

"Thanks. I think."

Mike hugs her.

"Have a good night. It's good to see you again," he said.

Jordan returned to her seat. "Sorry about that," she said, watching curiously as Mike walked away.

"Mike Postman," the boy responded admiringly. "He's a great guy."

"He has his moments," she said dryly.

He returned to see Kylie dancing by herself in the aisle. Mike loved the way she moved. Sweet, somewhat awkwardly, oblivious to the fact that nearly every straight, and possibly even a few gay males, were as enchanted by her as he was.

"Where'd you learn to dance? On the short bus?" Mike joked.

"I dance very well, thank you very much. And you love it."

He'd have been lying if he said he didn't.

"Why don't we get down closer to the stage?"

"How are we going to do that?"

"Trust me," he said as he took her hand.

"How bout letting us down front?" Mike asked the usher.

The man eyed him somewhat suspiciously.

"Do I know you from somewhere?" he asked.

This happened to Mike on a fairly regular basis. It was what he referred to as his "generic face".

Mike's lack of response only encouraged the man to continue. "I've seen you in something, haven't I?" the usher continued.

"You ever watch *Valerie*?" Tim interjected before Mike could answer.

"Sure, I've seen it."

Tim nodded towards Mike without saying a word.

"That's where I knew you from!" the man said enthusiastically. "How many are in your group?"

"Four," Tim said.

"Show your tickets to the guy over there," the man said. "He'll wave you through to the front."

"You don't look like Jason Bateman," Mike's sister said.

"Generic face strikes again," Mike answered.

"I take it this has happened before?" Kylie asked as they were whisked to the edges of the stage.

"People always think they know me. Their brother's friend. Their cousin's friend Vinny. Some guy from Long Island. Usually people want to fight me. This is the first time generic face has been used for good instead of evil," Mike said to Kylie's laughter.

A full day of school, a long ride to the concert, some alcohol, and a lot of dancing, left everyone exhausted enough that they were asleep as soon as their bottoms hit the car seats. Everyone that is, except for Tim, who was driving, and Mike, who was a pillow for Kylie. She had both of her arms wrapped around his waist and her head resting comfortably on his shoulder while she slept. That alone, vaulted this day to among his favorites of all time. He didn't even mind the puddle of drool that had formed on his shoulder.

"Thanks for inviting me tonight," Kylie said once they had returned to the neighborhood. "I had a great time."

"You're welcome. Thanks for coming," Mike answered. "You know, when I first got to school today, all Jimmy could talk about was how hot the new girl was. I was like, it's just Kylie."

"Gee. Thanks."

"I didn't mean it like that. It was just that he didn't recognize you."

"I didn't think he did," she laughed.

"He..." Mike hesitated, trying to find the right words, "wasn't entirely wrong."

"Entirely?! You sure know how to make a girl blush."

"You know what I mean," Mike said.

"Yeah. I'm not entirely repulsive."

"You're not repulsive at all."

"Stop. You're embarrassing me with all these compliments," she joked.

"Why do girls always have to take things the wrong way?" Mike pleaded.

"Maybe we wouldn't if guys knew how to say things the right way."

"You know you're cute. You don't need me to tell you that," Mike said at last.

"Did you just give me a compliment? Why Michael Postman, I don't think you've done that since I scored the winning touchdown in one of our football games when we were thirteen!"

"Call me tomorrow when you get up to your cousins," Mike said, embarrassed now.

"Oh, we're still going up tonight," Kylie answered. "Jeff's ready to leave. He said he took a nap earlier."

"Isn't it a little late? That's kind of a dark, winding drive."

"We're big people, Mikey Uptight," Kylie laughed. "But it's sweet of you to worry."

She kissed him on the lips because she knew he would have never done it on his own, and bounced across the lawn to her house. She was definitely cute. There was no arguing that.

As Mike walked up the stairs to his bedroom, he had a flashback, or a flash forward. In the confusion of the past several days, he wasn't sure which. It was of him waking up to his radio alarm to an announcer saying, "Tragedy last evening when two Milford teens were killed as they drove off the road in the Catskill Mountains. Brother and sister, Jeff and Kylie Peters were on their way to visit family in Watertown. Both were honor students and Kylie was an All-American soccer player who recently transferred to Allen's Creek Academy in Westport..."

Mike looked at his watch. Kylie had been killed at night when her brother had swerved down an embankment to avoid a deer on a mountain road.

He thought by bringing her to the concert this time, they wouldn't leave until the morning. Now that they were leaving anyway, he wasn't sure if things would be better, worse or the same. He decided not to take any chances.

He fired up his mother's car in the driveway and raced after them. They had about a two-minute head start. Looking ahead, he saw them in the distance, but knew he'd have to run a red light to catch up. He thought about it, but was forced to slam on his brakes   instead when a truck hurtled through the intersection.

"Damn it!" Mike screamed.

He turned down a side street, fishtailing as he went. He must have been going at least 70 down the alley, glancing over at the main drag every few seconds until he found himself running parallel to Kylie and her brother. He passed a car over a double line and skidded back onto the main road— directly in front of them. The last thing he remembered seeing was Kylie laughing at his heroics. She thought it was a game, until his car slid perilously close to the edge of the narrowing road—and eventually, off of it.

Mike's car rolled over and over and over again— four times in all—before settling to a crashing halt about forty feet down the hillside.

XII

~MANNY'S PLACE~

*M*ike and his father formed a close bond at an early age out of a mutual love of sports. The first present he ever received from his dad was a baseball glove. Follow up presents included a transistor radio and a baseball scorebook so he could keep score of every Mets game he listened to. He was six.

They made yearly pilgrimages to Cooperstown and the Baseball Hall of Fame, so Mike could get an official Mets cap, and run the bases at Doubleday Field. They went to Springfield, Massachusetts to the Basketball Hall of Fame and to Canton, Ohio to see the Pro Football Hall. They also attended a Sugar Bowl, an Orange Bowl, a Rose Bowl, an NCAA basketball Final 4, a NFL playoff game, a World Series game, and Willie Mays' last ever game. And while none of those would be considered unusual trips for a father and son to make, when they jumped in the car on Mike's 22nd birthday and drove to Iowa to see the cornfield where they filmed the movie, "Field of Dreams", his mother thought that was a bit excessive. But she never said a word, because you never wanted to interfere with the bond between a boy and his father.

And yet, of all the places they went. Of all the

games they attended.   One place consistently overshadowed the others.   Mike was six when he went his first Syracuse University football game. His father had attended Syracuse as both an undergrad and law student--his time there interrupted only by a two year stint as a radio gunner over Nagasaki during World War II—and Mike began to bleed orange and blue with him from the moment he stepped onto the campus.

He was at the last game ever played in ancient Archibold Stadium, taking a souvenir brick home with him after the game. He was at the first game ever played in the Carrier Dome. And he was at every "home away from home" game they played during the transition in between. They all started the same way, with his father blasting the Syracuse fight song over the stereo, mangling the words while he marched up and down the stairs of their home. A four hour drive ensued, getting them there in time for a quick sandwich on Marshall Street, before heading to Manny's.

Manny's had been a clothing store staple at the university for nearly 30 years. They carried every imaginable Syracuse t-shirt, sweatshirt, jacket, hat, pin, scarf, and rain poncho. The difficult part wasn't finding something you liked. It was deciding between them.

"Find something you want, Mikey?" Mr. Postman asked one fall afternoon.

Mike held up a navy sweatshirt with a bright orange "S" sewn across the chest, along with a matching hat.

"Not sure which one to get," Mike answered.

"The sweatshirt's pretty expensive."

"Don't worry about that. Which one do you like?"

"I don't know," he whined in the manner in which all parents of ten year olds were familiar.

"Well, you can't have a sweatshirt without a matching hat. So, let's get them both."

"Mom will get mad."

"Why would mom get mad?"

"Because she'll say I'm spoiled."

"The fact that you even think about that means there's a good possibility that you're not," his father said, taking both items from him.

"But what about mom?"

"You let me worry about your mother."

Turning to the man behind the counter he said, "We'll take them both."

The man was in his mid-seventies. Bald on top, with white hair on the sides and in back, he had kind eyes, a warm smile and a firm handshake. Manny had met his wife during World War I, moved back to her hometown, and opened his store in a small room above a bar on the same street where he now occupied half a block.

"We'll throw in the hat for free," Manny said.

"No, no no," Mr. Postman said, "but thank you. You have a business to run."

"You'll buy something next week."

"Next week is Penn State. Yes, we will."

Manny hadn't gotten to where he was without recognizing his best customers. Mike always felt as though his dad and Manny had a certain kinship. He wasn't sure if it was because they were both always immaculately dressed--button-down shirt, blazer, tie, spit-shined penny loafers—or because their upbeat demeanor masked the atrocities both saw during their respective Wars to End All Wars.

"Can I get a picture of you guys with dad?" a man asked. "We're trying to make a collection for our back wall."

Manny's son was about Mr. Postman's age, and the spitting image of his father. Manny and Mr. Postman stood with their arms around each other like old friends, with Mike in front of them, wearing both of his new purchases. It looked like something out of a Norman Rockwell painting.

Stepping outside into the autumn air, Mike was reminded why he loved going to the games so much. The smell of people grilling hot dogs and sausages. Frisbees and footballs flying through the air. And while the sight of thousands of inebriated 30-somethings trying to relive their college years, might have been intimidating to most ten year olds, Mike was amused by them.

The game itself was the main event and they stayed until the final whistle no matter what the score, the weather, or time of day.

"The one time we leave, is the time we'll miss something great," Mike once told his father.

So they never left early. Not once.

Their post game meal was eaten at the same Italian restaurant, with the same waitress, wearing the same uniform as she had for the past twenty years. Of course they ate the same meal. Spaghetti with meat sauce and a salad with Italian dressing and crumbled blue cheese. The Postman men were not known for change. Then it was back in the car for the four-hour ride home. Mike would always try to stay awake to keep his father company on the ride back to no avail. He father usually carried him into the house around midnight.

As the years passed, their trips to Syracuse became less frequent since Mike had games of his own to play. His father rarely missed one of them. A fixture on the sideline with the transistor radio he had given Mike so many years ago, he would listen to the Syracuse game while watching his son, occasionally shouting out the score as Mike ran past. When Mike went off to college, and eventually, when he moved to California, they would speak after every Syracuse football and basketball game—celebrating if they won, and critiquing them if they lost. Some seasons, there was more critiquing going on than celebrating. Other years, it was the other way around. But after years of hearing his father talk about 1959, the year Syracuse won the National Championship in football, he used to pray that his father would live to see them win another one in either football or basketball.

When Mike's father was 78 years old, it finally happened. A freshman, future NBA superstar, led an otherwise unheralded Syracuse basketball team to the National Championship in true Cinderella fashion. Ironically, that was the same year and month of the big ice storm that knocked out power in large portions of New England for nearly a week, so Mike's mom and dad had to watch the game in a hotel. Mike himself was watching some 3,000 miles away, but for the last 10 minutes, they watched together via the phone. A week later, Mike returned home for a visit, but had to make one stop before he got there. It took him four hours each way to do it, but his dad was well worth the trip.

Mike hadn't stepped foot in Manny's in more than 15 years, but it hadn't changed a bit, except that it was largely empty on a weekday afternoon, save for the man behind the counter. Manny was long since gone, having passed away twelve years earlier at the ripe old age of 90. His son owned the place now and he was the only person working when Mike walked in.

"Can I help you find something?" Manny Jr. asked.

"I'm looking for something for my dad. Something to commemorate the championship."

Manny Jr. eyed Mike a bit more closely now, as if there was something familiar about him that he couldn't quite place.

"Well, we have this trophy basketball, signed by all members of the team, that also lists the game and score for each game they played in the tournament."

"That's really nice," Mike said. "My dad would like that."

He then spotted an old style letterman's jacket hanging on the wall. "Now, *that* he would love," he said, pointing to it. "The coach wanted him to play football here, but he had to work in order to put himself through college. Tell you what. I'll take them both."

Manny Jr. smiled and wrapped them up for him. Behind the cash register a framed story and photograph caught Mike's eye.

"That's what they wrote about my dad in the Post Standard the day after he died," Manny Jr. said when he noticed Mike staring at it. "The people with him in the picture were a father and son who used to come in before every—"

And that's when he placed him. Mike smiled shyly as if he was ten all over again.

"That was you and your dad?" Manny Jr. half stated and half asked.

Mike reached into his wallet and pulled out the identical photograph. "Your father found our address on one of our receipts and mailed a copy to us years ago."

"My father used to look forward to seeing you guys each week. Your dad helped build this place," he laughed. "It's been a long time."

"My dad doesn't travel much anymore," Mike explained. "And I've been living in California."

Manny Jr. placed the ball and jacket into an oversized bag. "On the house," he said.

"No, no, no."

Manny Jr. handed him the bag. He wasn't taking no for an answer. "Tell your father hello."

OCTOBER 25, 1986

DAY 3

XIII

~A SLOW ROLLER UP THE 1^(ST) BASE LINE~

*M*ike opened his eyes slowly, one at a time. He staggered to the bathroom and seemed surprised to not find one visible cut or scratch on his entire body when he looked in the mirror. He pulled out a bottle of Tylenol and swallowed two of them without water just as his father walked into the room.

"I'll be back at four, Mike. We have to catch the 4:20 train if we're going to make first pitch," his father said.

"First pitch?"

"World Series. Game Six. Shea Stadium. Tonight. Any of that ringing a bell?"

"My head is killing me."

"You overdo it with the boys last night?" his father asked.

"Mom's car. I wrecked it."

"Yeah. Three years ago. And you've been paying her back ever since. Man, you must have really tied one on last night. I'm glad you weren't driving."

"And Kylie?" Mike asked.

"Is coming with us to the game. You invited her. Remember?" his father said, shaking his head.

When Kylie rang their doorbell at 3:55 that afternoon, Mike was completely torn about what to do. On one hand, he wanted desperately to hug her, to tell her all the things he never got to the first time around. On the other, he wasn't sure how that would be received. After all, he had no idea whether they were dating, just friends, or in that grey area somewhere in between.

"How are you, Ky?" he asked as he attempted to mask his excitement.

"Are we going to win tonight?" she responded.

"Definitely. No question about it," Mike said confidently. That was one thing he was certain of.

Four and a half hours later, Kylie found herself sitting in the upper deck of Shea Stadium, with her elbows on her knees, her head resting in her open palms. Her Mets hat was inside out and backwards, while her jersey was unbuttoned three quarters of the way down. Adorable would have been the most underrated word to describe her in Mike's eyes.

The scoreboard read "Boston 5 New York 3" with two outs in the bottom of the 10th inning.

"You guys want to head out of here and beat the traffic?" Mr. Postman asked.

"We never leave early, dad," Mike answered.

"You're right, you're right," his father agreed.

Kylie didn't respond at all, merely raising her eyebrows only slightly when Gary Carter singled on the next pitch. After Kevin Mitchell followed with another single, she sat up in her seat defiantly, almost as if to say she knew they were teasing her. When Ray Knight singled home Carter to make it 5-4, Kylie rose to her feet along with the rest of the stadium.

"Come on Mook-ie! Let's go Mook-ster!" she screamed, suddenly coming to life.

By the time Mookie Wilson jumped out of the way to avoid a wild pitch, allowing Mitchell to score, she was standing on her seat.

Although it was close, Mike was pretty sure he enjoyed watching her reaction to the comeback even more than he had enjoyed seeing it himself the first time around—especially after she ended up in his arms once Mookie's slow roller got past Bill Buckner and the Mets won. His father even managed to get a kiss on the cheek from a seventy-five year old lady in the row in front of them.

"What an incredible game!" Kylie exclaimed spinning around in circles in very tight quarters while everyone waited for the subway to arrive.

No one seemed seemed to mind.

"They're going to be talking about this one for years to come."

"They certainly will," Mike assured her.

The doors opened on the arriving car and everyone piled in. When the mob threatened to separate them all, Mike grabbed her hand, and pulled her close to him.

"Are you going to tell Megan you brought me here?" she whispered, her head resting on his shoulder.

"Why wouldn't I?"

"I don't know. Maybe because she already hates me."

Mike was glad she had used a name, because otherwise he would have had no idea whom he was actually dating. It turned out to be the same girl he had dated in college the first time around. They had broken up two weeks after graduation because they wanted different things in life. He didn't see it lasting even that long this time.

"She doesn't hate you. And what about you? Are you going to tell your boyfriend?" He didn't even know his name.

"We broke up yesterday," Kylie said.

"Open mouth, insert foot," Mike answered. "I'm sorry."

"Don't be," she said. "He was a Red Sox fan."

"Well, I'm sure it will only be a matter of time before guys start banging down your door for a date."

"I don't know about that."

"There's someone for everyone, Ky."

"Do you really believe that?" she asked.

"Why? Are you worried you're becoming an old maid?"

"Not exactly," she laughed.

"That's good, because you still have at least one or two good years left in you before you're over the hill."

"You're six months older than me, pal."

"Yeah, but everyone knows men age far more gracefully than women," Mike said.

"Says who?"

"Robert Redford, Tom Cruise, Harrison Ford and Kevin Costner. Name an attractive older woman."

"Demi Moore."

"I'll give you Demi Moore, and maybe Christie Brinkley, but that's about it. As the saying goes, 'You can look old or you can look weird, but you can't look young, no matter how much plastic surgery you have."

"Whatever."

"Just accept it. In a few years, you'll be twice as old as me."

"Maybe maturity wise," she answered.

"Touche'," he said. "But in answer to your question, the romantic in me thinks there has to be someone for everyone. The problem is, life is so damn complicated, it's not all that easy to find that person. I guess fate plays a part. But I also think if you're one of the lucky ones who is able to make a connection, you had better not let anyone or anything get in the way."

"And how do you know when you've found that person?" she asked, intrigued.

"I think you just know. The person will have all the qualities you're looking for."

"And what are you looking for?"

"First of all, when there's absolutely nothing exciting going on in the world—which is most of the time—I'll still enjoy being around her, even if we're just sitting there talking. And secondly, and probably most importantly, the right person for me will have to be very kind. She'll have a heart of gold."

"That's really sweet. Does Megan have those two qualities?"

"I think so," he said. "But sometimes I think someone else might have those qualities even more. If that makes any sense."

An uncomfortable silence followed. Kylie wasn't sure if he was talking about her, and Mike didn't know what her reaction would be if she knew he was.

"So, back to college in the morning, huh?" she said at last as he walked her to her door.

"My roommate is supposed to pick me up on his way back from Boston, but after tonight's game, it wouldn't surprise me if he just drove straight through Connecticut."

"It would be hard to blame him."

"You should come visit me during your trimester break," Mike said.

"And what would Megan say about that?"

"She'd probably be furious. But I've known you my entire life. If she can't understand that we're friends, then that's her problem. Speaking of Megan, I was supposed to call her about an hour ago."

"Is that what we are? Friends?" Kylie asked.

"About that," Mike began. "I've been meaning to talk to you."

"What about?" she asked. She wasn't about to let him off the hook easily.

"About...being more than that," he stammered.

"I don't know, Mikey. This coming from the guy who told me he'd rather go drinking with his buddies than take me to the Senior Prom."

"That was a long time ago," Mike said defensively.

"It was a year and a half ago," she exclaimed.

"Well, I've matured a lot since then."

"Yes, it seemed like it when you were throwing peanut shells in the hood of the old woman in front of us at the game," she laughed.

"I didn't want to litter."

"Why don't you go call Megan and then call me

tomorrow?" Kylie said. "That way, I'll know it wasn't the euphoria of the Mets game talking."

"I'll do that," he said. "At least I hope I'll do that," he said to himself as he headed across the lawn to his house.

XIV

˜DARK CLOUDS FALLING FROM
THE SKY˜

The impact of 9/11 was so far reaching and absolute, that it was difficult to find someone who hadn't been affected by it in some manner. Some lost relatives. Others lost friends. Or friends of friends. Or work colleagues. One thing was certain. Everyone felt a little more vulnerable because of it. We were attacked on our own soil in a more devastating fashion than Pearl Harbor. Five hundred more people were killed, nearly all of them innocent civilians.

Todd Pelligrino was an investment broker working for Cantor-Fitzgerald in the North Tower of the Trade Center at the time of the attacks. His day had begun just like nearly every other September morning. Sunny, blue skies. Temperatures warming into the mid-70's . The difference on this day was that September 11th, also happened to be the first day of school for his six year old son. He wanted desperately to be the one dropping him off at school, but a need to be in the office before the market opened made that impossible.

At 8:00am, he called to wish his son good luck.

Forty-five minutes later, he called his wife back to tell her that an explosion had occurred in the building and he was going to try and get out. "I love you" were the last words he spoke to her before hanging up the phone. He was never heard from again.

When news of Todd's story hit the Connecticut Post about a week or so later, Irene Postman clipped out the story, and mailed it to her son in California. Mike had grown up playing soccer with Todd Pelligrino on various town teams from the time they were six. They were fast friends back then. Mike liked that Todd was nearly always smiling; nearly always in a good mood. And while a number of Mike's other friends distanced themselves from him once he decided to stay at his private school, rather than returning and playing soccer with them at the public one, Todd never did. And although time and distance over the years had made maintaining a friendship difficult, news of Todd's passing left a definite void—as if a chip of his childhood had disappeared with him.

The newspaper article sat underneath the glass on Mike's desk as a constant reminder of how fleeting life could be but also that a friendship wasn't about how often you saw or spoke to someone, as much as how you felt about them when you did.

SEPTEMBER 11, 2001

DAY 4

XV

~EVEN THE BEST LAID PLANS...~

The clock on Mike's nightstand changed over from 6:29 to 6:30am and a haranguing buzzing sound commenced. In one deft motion, Mike swatted the clock to the floor, before he climbed from his bed with a sense of urgency.

After splashing some cold water on his face, he looked into the mirror and saw that he had aged fifteen years overnight. It didn't bother him much. It seemed far more normal than looking into the mirror and seeing a teenager staring back at him, which is what he had done for the past three mornings. *That* had unnerved him.

Mike went into his closet and sifted through the boxes on the shelf and floor, but didn't find what he was looking for. He continued his search in every other closet and room in the house, becoming more frantic with each unsuccessful foray, before he finally picked up the phone.

The phone rang on the other end until his parents' answering machine picked up. He decided it best not to waste anymore time. What he was looking for *had* to be at their house. He made the seven minute drive in four minutes.

Mike didn't bother to knock, but used his spare key instead and wound up startling his bathrobe-wearing mother in the kitchen while she poured a cup of coffee.

"My God, you scared the devil out of me!" she exclaimed.

"I called," Mike answered absently as he raced up the stairs.

He tore his old room apart, throwing things randomly around the room and to the floor of his closet. Nothing.

"What is the matter with you?!" his mother asked.

"Where are my baseball cards?" he demanded.

"They're in the attic. Why are you acting like such a maniac? And don't you have school?"

"Can't explain now," he said, brushing past her.

He pulled down the stairs and scaled them with the purpose of a mountain climber. His parents' attic was neater and more organized than most business showrooms. Everything was labeled and separated by person. The far right corner contained Mike's personal items. There was only one box he was concerned about. A shoebox. When his eyes settled on it, he breathed a barely perceptible sigh of relief, but only for an instant.

Inside it were baseball cards, some more than thirty years old. All the big names were there. Willie Mays. Hank Aaron. Pete Rose. Folded up neatly in between Willie Stargell and Tom Seaver was the piece of paper he had written on twenty-one years earlier, although it seemed like only three days ago to him. He was relieved it was still there. But of course it wouldbe. He would never have thrown out his baseball cards. They were a link to his childhood.

He dialed 411 on his cell phone. "Boston, Massachusetts," he said. "The Federal Bureau of Investigation."

He waited impatiently for the operator to connect him, alternately sitting and standing every few seconds.

"Is this the emergency line?" he asked at last. "Good. I'm not sure who else to turn to, but I need to report four potential hijackings this morning. Two out of Logan Airport in Boston. One out of Dulles. And one out of Newark, New Jersey. No, this is not a crank call. This is deadly serious."

There was a slight pause on the other end of the line. He realized how unbelievable that must have sounded to someone pre-9/11.

"My name is Michael Postman. I live in Woodmont, Connecticut and no, I'm not affiliated in any way with the hijackings. I just know they're going to happen," he continued. "How? I'm psychic," he said. "I can tell you anything major that will happen in the next ten years, and I am telling you that you need to stop these planes from taking off. I can give you airlines, flight numbers and even the last names of the hijackers," he said, laying the sheet of paper out in front of him. They didn't seem to be taking him seriously, and he couldn't help but wonder what the worst thing would be if they acted and he was wrong? A few wasted phone calls and a couple hundred inconvenienced travelers? Why must people in a position to do something act so idiotic?

He paced back and forth. "You can question me until the cows come home," he said. "I've got nothing to hide. You can find me at Monroe High

School, in Monroe, Connecticut where I teach. My home address is 107 Marx Street, as in the singer. Woodmont, Connecticut. My cell number is (203) 555-9164. Feel free to trace it. Now, listen to me carefully," he continued, "Get out a piece of paper and write this information down. American Airlines. Flight 11 from Boston to Los Angeles. Scheduled departure time is 7:45am—are you writing this down?? The hijackers last names are Atta. A-t-t-a. al-Shehri. a-l dash capital S-h-e-h-r-i. Two of them have that last name. al-Omari. a-l dash capital O-m-a-r-i. And al-Suqami. That's a-l dash capital S-u-q-a-m-i. Check with the airlines. Those names will be on the list as passengers for that flight. They will hijack that plane with box cutter knives that they will smuggle on, and they will run that plane into the North Tower of the World Trade Center. No, this is not some sort of sick joke. Next plane," he continued, then paused, "Are you really writing this down or pretending to? United Airlines flight 175. Also from Boston to Los Angeles. Search and arrest passengers, al-Shehhi, Banihammad, al-Shehri, and two passengers with the last name al-Ghamdi. They're the only guys of Arab decent on the flight. This plane will head to the South Tower of the World Trade Center."

There was another long pause and Mike raised his eyebrows. "Look, we're running out of time. Some of these guys may already be through security. There are two more flights. American Airlines flight 77 from Dulles. And United Airlines flight 93 from Newark. If you give me a fax number, I'll fax over all the names and information."

Mike jumped down the attic stairs and raced to his father's office. He punched in the number as they gave it to him. "Call the FAA, the Pentagon, whoever you have to call," he continued. "but...ground...these...flights!" Another pause. "Ask yourself one question. How would I possibly know these people are on all of these flights? That information is not given out. Besides, if I'm wrong and the flights are delayed an hour, who cares?! Flights are always late. And then you can come arrest me. But if I'm right, and you don't do anything about it, two-thousand, nine-hundred and seventy four people are going to die today," he said as he hung up.

He wasn't convinced they believed him. He called information once again. "The World Trade Center. Main Switchboard," he said. "Listen carefully," he began after a slight pause, "There are bombs in both the North and South Towers. You need to evacuate the buildings immediately. The bombs are on the 5th floor," Mike said before hanging up.

He was sweating now, and unsure of what to do next. He called both American and United Airlines and told them they each had flights that would be hijacked. He didn't feel as though anyone was taking him seriously. Prior to 9/11, no one could have fathomed such a breach of security could ever take place.

Mike sprinted past his parents yelling, "I'll call you!" as he did. He drove home obeying not a single traffic law along the way, and took a lightning fast shower. If he was going to be arrested, he at least wanted to be clean. He arrived at the school at 7:25. First bell rang five minutes later.

"You guys have worksheets to complete today," he said to the class as he handed them out. "Just do them quietly."

He turned on the television in the room, but there was no news coverage. Only Matt Lauer and Katie Couric.

At 7:37am, twenty Federal agents, armed to the teeth, pulled in front of Monroe High School in four Chevy Suburbans and three Crown Victorias. Mike knew immediately who they were there to see.

"Chrissy. Go down to the main office and tell them they need to find someone to cover the rest of my classes today," he said to a girl in the front row.

Mike met the agents outside the entrance, and was quickly cuffed and shoved into the back of one of the Suburbans while hundreds of stunned students looked on through the windows of the building.

"Where are we going?" Mike asked any of the four agents in the van with him who cared to respond.

Navy suits, earpieces, sunglasses. Agents Jackson, Johnson, Jones and Jermain looked like they had just stepped off the set of the next *Men in Black* sequel.

"Hartford," Agent Jackson replied. "And you had better start making some sense, Mike."

"I've already told you everything I know," Mike answered, his palms in the air for added emphasis. "Have you stopped the flights?"

"We've detained the five men at Dulles and the

four at Newark."

"What about Boston? Those are the most important ones."

"The men were already through security by the time we got the information to them," Agent Jones answered. "But they're stopping them at the gate."

"Why don't you just ground the flight?!" Mike exclaimed.

"Do you have any idea what's involved in doing that?" Agent Johnson asked.

"No. Nor do I care."

"We should be getting confirmation that we have them any moment now," Agent Jackson said. "What we need to know is how you're involved in all this."

"I'm not involved," Mike said. "If I was involved, would I be trying to prevent it?"

"Maybe you're a mercenary, and they double crossed you, and this is your way of getting even."

"Look. Go to my house. Tear it upside down. Search my computer. Go through my underwear drawer," Mike urged. "You won't find anything except some baseball cards and maybe a Playboy or two."

A cell phone rang. Agent Jackson answered it. "Yes," he said. "What?! Call it back then! I understand. You need to call the Pentagon."

"What happened?!" Mike asked.

"They stopped the ones on the United Airlines flight, but there was a mix up with the American flight and it had already left the gate by the time they arrived," he said, concerned now for the first time.

"Call it back!"

"They tried to, but the hijackers took over the

plane on the ramp. The plane just lifted off."

"Oh my god," Mike said.

"Can we shoot it down?" Agent Jones asked.

"It will probably take too long to get our planes off the ground and find them, but they're going to try," Jackson replied.

"This won't help the passengers on board," Mike said, "But on the chance you didn't believe me or weren't able to stop them, I called in a bomb threat to the Trade Center. Both Towers should be evacuated by now."

"You told them the bomb was on the 5th floor," Agent Jackson said.

"Yes. So police wouldn't go searching the entire building and get caught above where the plane would hit."

"In case of a bomb threat on the lower floors, they keep everyone more than twenty-five floors up in their offices, so they don't risk getting caught on the way out. The buildings were built to sustain bomb damage thirty floors up. It would take a nuclear bomb to bring the building down."

"Or a jet plane with 24,000 gallons of fuel," Mike said. "Tell them to evacuate the building. There is no bomb. They've only got twenty minutes to do it. The plane will hit at 8:46."

At 8:31, they pulled into FBI Headquarters in Hartford. All television stations were now tuned to the rapidly evacuating World Trade Center towers as people poured from the buildings. Mike had to strain to see the television through the window in the interrogation room they had left him in.

At 8:46, Mike closed his eyes and winced as he

listened to the reaction in the other room. The plane hit the North Tower just above the 94th floor. There were no words to adequately describe the emotion of experiencing 9/11 again. The first time he had been teaching when a student ran into his classroom to tell him a plane had hit the Trade Center. His first thought, like so many others, was that an errant Cessna, flown by an inexperienced pilot, had veered off course and glanced off the building. But seeing the horrors of a landmark building in flames, with people leaping to their death 100 floors up, followed by the buildings collapsing in heaps of twisted and melted metal, left indelible images in Mike's mind that he would never be able to fully erase.

After four more hours of repetitive questioning, they brought Mike back to his house, where they proceeded to turn it upside down, just as he had suggested. They found nothing of course—except for some baseball cards and a couple of *Playboys.* One of the agents took one as evidence.

"We'll need you to surrender your passport," Agent Jackson said.

"I don't have a passport," Mike answered. "I haven't left the country since I was sixteen."

"Well, don't leave the area," Jackson continued.

Mike collapsed onto what remained of his couch as soon as they left. He had closed his eyes for a split second before the phone rang. "Hello," he answered.

"Michael. Have you been watching the news?"

"Yes, Mom, but I'm kind of tired right now. Can I call you back?"

"Kylie was at work in the Trade Center," she said. "The one that was hit."

"They evacuated the building," Mike said. "I thought everyone got out."

"Most did, but there are still a few people that haven't been accounted for."

"Oh my god," Mike said. He wasn't sure how much more he could take. "I take it her parents have tried reaching her on her cell?"

"Most cell service went out after the plane hit. The lines are all jammed."

"I'm going down there," Mike said at last. "I'll be in touch as soon as I find her. And I will find her."

All public transportation and roads into the city were closed for 25 miles in every direction. Mike had to park in Co-op City and continue the journey into lower Manhattan on foot.

He arrived just before sunrise, but the closest he was allowed was five blocks from the site. Dust and soot was on every street corner and floating in the air. He wasn't even sure what he was doing there. Finding Kylie in the chaos would be more difficult than finding a needle in a haystack. But he couldn't just do nothing. He called out her name for what felt like helpless hours, but his voice was drowned out by the sounds of fire trucks, police sirens and jackhammers coming from the site.

Exhausted and drained, Mike sat down on the front steps of an old church that was doubling as a homeless shelter, leaned back against a pillar, and closed his eyes.

OCTOBER 17, 2011

DAY 5

XVI

˜THE END OF THE END˜

*M*ike woke up on a couch in the faculty lounge at the high school.

"Sleeping already and the day hasn't even started yet," an older teacher said with a smile. "Or did you sleep here?"

Mike looked in the mirror and determined that it was possible. The stack of graded papers next to him confirmed it.

"I had a ton of papers to grade. Knew I'd be up late, so I figured I would work here and get a few hours of sleep. Showered in the gym locker room."

"Sure you showered?"

He took a quick sniff of his armpits and suddenly wasn't so sure anymore.

The calendar on the wall read, "October, 17, 2011". Mike sat down at a computer and Googled 9/11. Ninety-seven people died that day. 92 on the plane that hit the tower, plus five who didn't get out in time. Sad, most definitely, but a far cry from the nearly three thousand that had been killed before. The question he had was whether Kylie had been one of them. He Googled her name, but nothing came up. He would have to continue his search later.

Mike left the lounge and saw Lisa Wolper and a couple of her friends standing by their lockers.

"Just getting here, ladies?" he asked.

"Well, Mr. Postman, it's amazing I made it here at all considering I didn't wake up until almost 5:30 today," one of the other girls answered.

Kim Devine wasn't the sharpest knife in the drawer, but she was one of the prettiest. The Captain of the cheerleading squad, she had the brunette, Barbie doll looks that were a combination of natural beauty and several hours of daily primping.

"5:30?!" Mike said, "The last time these eyes saw 5:30 was after seeing every hour in between, because I hadn't gone to sleep the night before. School doesn't start until 7:30. Why so early?"

"Oh my god, I have to curl my hair," she answered.

"That should take until about 5:35."

"I have to put on my makeup."

"5:40."

"I have to decide on an outfit."

"5:41."

"Are you kidding? I have to look nice."

"I'm sure you'd look just as nice in half the time."

"I might as well kill myself if that's true," she answered.

"That might be a bit of an extreme reaction," Mike said.

A male student walked up and joined the conversation.

"All I know is that it took me five minutes to get

ready this morning. About as long as it took me to get ready for the prom. And I look mah-ve-lous."

"That's cause you're a guy," Kim said. "You can get away with rolling out of bed and putting on a baseball cap."

"You're a pretty girl, Kim," Mike said. "You don't need to waste all that time getting ready. Spend it doing your Algebra homework."

"Yeah, right. If I just rolled out of bed and came to school, no one would speak to me."

"It's all in how you carry yourself. If you like yourself, so will everyone else. There's more to Kim Devine than a few curls and some eyeliner."

"My mother always tells me to make sure I look nice. She says the minute I don't, a man will dump me."

"Your mother's a sharp lady," the boy interjected.

Lisa joined the conversation. "My mother married my great uncle," she said.

"She married your father's uncle?!" Mike asked incredulously.

"No. My great uncle *is* my father. My mom married *her* uncle."

"Are you serious?"

"No, I'm not serious, Mr. Postman. Do you think we all sleep with our relatives up here?"

"Well...that would explain some things," Mike cracked.

Standing quietly the entire time was Lisa Hunter. She was pretty as well, with sandy blond hair, and delicate features. She was clearly the most conservative of the three.

"I have to get my chocolate fix," Lisa Wolper said. "I've been having a craving for it. Mr. Postman, will you be around later? I need to talk to you about something."

"You know where my room is," he said, before turning to the other Lisa. "You ok, L2?"

"Yes," she answered quietly.

Mike leaned against the lockers. "You sure?"

Years of teaching had given him the ability to read students' minds. He knew not only that there was something wrong, but that if he waited long enough, eventually she would tell him about it.

"It's just that all anyone talks about is food and eating," she blurted out at last. "They're always telling me I don't eat enough."

"And do you?"

"I haven't eaten anything other than a few carrots a day and diet soda for three weeks."

She didn't seem to be trying to impress. Merely was stating a fact.

"That doesn't sound very healthy," Mike said. "How come you're not eating?"

"I'm never very hungry," she answered. "My mother and my sister know about it. They try to force me to eat. My grandmother cried the other day because she thought I was too skinny."

"And what do you think?"

"I think I still need to lose a few more pounds."

"It's not my place to tell you what to do, but maybe you should see a doctor to make sure you're healthy."

"I've already been to one," Lisa said. "He told me if I lose five more pounds, he's going to check me into the hospital."

"Well, out of all the people you talk to, including me, the doctor is the one person you should trust the most. Because everything he tells you is based on what is healthy, and not an opinion of what looks good."

"I guess," she answered at barely above a whisper.

"Sometimes, L2, it's easier to hit a problem head-on, rather than letting it sneak up on you later."

"I know. And everyone keeps telling me I'm skinny, but when I look in the mirror, I see someone who's fat and ugly."

"That's why I would listen to your doctor. It's his job to give you an objective opinion," he said as he patted her on the back. "Let me know if there's anything I can do," he added.

"Thanks, Mr. P."

Mike entered his classroom and found a lone boy seated at a desk near the front. Bill DiPoto was clean-cut and athletic, but like so many people his age—shy until he got to know you. Mike didn't seem surprised to see him.

"So, I hear you're in the process of flunking yourself off the football team," Mike began.

"Big deal," Bill answered.

"You don't care?"

"I'm not having any fun anyway. Coach McNeil hasn't been playing me."

"That's probably because he knows you're about to become ineligible."

"But I'm not yet. He just likes to bust my balls," Bill said.

"Here's the thing, Bill. And there's really no way around it. Why should Coach play you now, when he knows that in two weeks when he really needs you, you won't be eligible?"

Bill shrugged. He didn't have an answer for that one.

"From what I understand, you're failing because you're not trying. Why should he rely on someone who doesn't even care enough about the team to keep himself eligible?"

Bill looked away. "Whatever."

Mike sat down on the edge of the teacher's desk. "Let me put it this way. Forget football. Forget your parents. Forget your teachers. If someone gave you a new pair of Nike's, or an IPhone, or an IPad, you wouldn't let anyone steal it from you, and you wouldn't walk over and toss it in the trashcan. Am I right?"

"What's your point?"

"My point is that an education is far more valuable than any of those things. An education is what is going to enable you to buy those things and other things like them, later in life. It's the most valuable thing anyone will ever give you for free. It's stupid to throw it away."

"I guess," Bill admitted begrudgingly. "But high school sucks. They don't let us get away with anything."

"They don't let you guys get away with anything because they know you'd take advantage of it if they did. If you guys were deserving of more freedom, you'd probably get it."

"It wouldn't matter how we acted."

"I think you'd be surprised," Mike said. "Twenty years ago, when I was in high school, they were much more lenient with us. They let us sign out during free periods, and walk through the halls without a pass."

"You see, that's cool."

"They let us do those things because we had respect for authority."

"Sounds like you guys were geeks," Bill said.

"We weren't geeks," Mike answered defensively. "We had our skip days and our prank days."

"Last year, our seniors let five live chickens loose during the Honors Assembly."

"I remember," Mike said.

"And then a couple of guys dropped some acid in Mr. Webster's coffee mug."

"I remember that as well. But what was funny about that?"

"It was funny when he started hallucinating and passed out in the middle of the room," Bill laughed.

"That's not funny. That's cruel."

"What did you guys do for pranks? Not wear socks?"

Mike walked across the room musing, "What did we do? Well, my senior year, we broke into the school and filled the principal's office from ceiling to floor with balloons. You couldn't even step inside it by the time we were done."

"That's pretty cool. What did he say?"

"He asked for a safety pin," Mike laughed. "For an encore, we took all of the furniture out of the cafeteria and put it on the roof. We set it up exactly the way it had been inside. The students of Allen's

Creek Academy ate lunch on the roof that day."

"How'd you break in?"

"Someone stole a key. It got passed on from class to class."

"I wonder if we could get a hold of a key?" Bill thought out loud.

"They'd probably have you arrested," Mike said.

"You see, that's the thing. You went to a private school. It's different."

"It's different only in that kids were different back then. Even at the public schools. We had more respect for teachers, and I'm not just saying that because I'm one of them. We still screwed around and had fun, but it was more good-natured. It wasn't cruel or destructive."

Bill didn't respond, probably because he knew Mike was right. But what appeared to be a moment of reason and understanding, suddenly turned to chaos. Screams in the hallway caused Mike to race from the room with a start.

"J.R. just hit a girl!" a student yelled.

"Is she ok?" Mike yelled after him.

"She hit her head. An ambulance is on the way."

"Shit," Mike said as he followed the student down the hall.

He arrived in the front lobby just in time to see a handcuffed student shoved into the back of a police cruiser. He waded his way through the crowd until he found a fellow teacher.

"What happened?" Mike asked.

"Apparently they had some words," the teacher said. "The girl insulted his mother, and he gave her a shove."

"Is she going to be all right?"

"I think so. She bumped her head pretty good, so they're taking her to the hospital as a precaution."

"I can't say that I'm surprised," Mike said.

A school administrator approached the two of them. Jim Banelli was the Director of Special Education at the school. He was friendly to your face, but made you feel as though the other shoe could drop at any moment. The expression on Mike's face made it clear he wasn't a big fan.

"What happened?" Jim asked.

"J.R. shoved a girl to the ground. They just arrested him," Mike answered coldly.

"You're kidding."

"No, I'm not. Nor was I kidding three months ago when I told you he shouldn't be allowed in this school."

Mike began to walk away. Jim followed him.

"Mike, we need to talk."

"What about?" he answered without breaking stride.

"About what you're going to say when people start asking you questions about J.R."

"The same thing I told you when you had an intern walking him to my class. That any kid who couldn't be trusted to walk the halls alone, shouldn't be allowed in the school in the first place."

"He's made a lot of progress," Jim said.

"Look, I'm all for giving kids a second chance. And even a third one if necessary. But you and I both know the only reason you let him stay in school is because you were afraid his big shot parents would sue the district if you didn't. Kind of ironic that you're probably going to get sued anyway," Mike said.

"I think what you should say, is that J.R. had been making progress, but took a step backward today."

"Is that what you think?"

"The school cannot afford the bad publicity a messy law suit would generate."

"I don't give a damn what the school can or cannot afford. The *reason* kids don't value education is because you don't make it a privilege. You give it to anyone, no matter how undeserving. And furthermore, the *school* should have thought about that before they let you put your own political agenda ahead of the best interests of the kids."

"That's not fair," Jim said.

Mike finally stopped walking and turned to face him. "You're right. It's not fair. For the kids."

Mike reentered his classroom just before the bell rang. He grabbed his attendance sheet from his desk and noticed immediately that the clipping of his friend who had been killed in 9/11 wasn't there.

"Let's see who's here today," he said to the class at last. "Mr. Hicks. Mr. Jones. Ronan the Barbarian."

Miss Ronan smiled shyly and shook her head.

"Mr. Postman. Why do you always make fun of Kristin?" Miss Doyle asked.

"Because it's so easy, Miss Doyle," Mike responded.

"That's not very nice."

"I never claimed to be nice, Miss Doyle. Besides, I've missed it."

"Since yesterday?"

Mike smiled. "Yes. Since yesterday. It seems like a lot longer."

Miss Spazato quietly entered the room.

"Ah, Miss Spazato, nice of you to find time for us in your busy schedule. Good to see you. Thanks for dropping by today."

"No problem," she smiled.

In the back of the room and right on cue, Mr. Phillips knocked Mr. Mulligan's book off his desk. "Well, as soon as Mr. Phillips and Mr. Mulligan are finished playing grab-ass, we can get started," Mike announced.

The class roared, followed by a soft knock on the door that was only audible once they had quieted down. Lisa Wolper entered. She didn't say a word. She didn't have to. Mike knew the conversation that was about to take place.

He walked into the parking lot a couple of hours later, and removed the keys from his pocket. They were on a Porsche key chain. He nodded with self-approval and began hitting the lock button until he heard a car beep a row away. It was a 911 Carrera. He nodded again. Life was good. A few hours later, Mike found himself back at the shoreline, walking along the Long Island Sound; a million thoughts racing through his head. Was Kylie alive? Had he made a difference in anyone's life? What was going to happen to him at the end of *this* day?

Once again, he heard the distant shouts of the boy as he ran towards him.

"Mister! Mister! My friend just fell in off the pier and he can't swim! I'm not a good enough swimmer to pull him out! Can you help me?!" the boy screamed as he approached.

Mike kicked off his shoes and dove in off the pier. He reached the boy's friend, and began the task of pushing him toward the shore. He gave him one last shove toward safety before dropping beneath the surface once again. This time, however, he resurfaced seconds later, and took two giant strokes to get within a few feet of the pier. He managed to pull himself onto the deck after a struggle and collapsed into a puddle of water.

"Are you ok, mister?" the first boy asked.

He thought about it for a second before answering, "Yeah. I'm ok."

"You're an idiot!" the first boy said to the second. "I told you the water was deep."

The other boy punched him and within moments, they were laughing about the near death experience. That's how little boys were.

Mike dried himself off with a towel from the back of his car and changed his clothes before driving home. He was surprised to find that his house was no longer grey, but a rather bright green instead. The very sight of it made him cringe.

His key fit into the lock, but it wouldn't turn. He tried a few others as well, only to be startled when a man opened the door from the inside. "What the hell are you doing?!" the man wanted to know.

"What are you doing in my house?!" Mike responded defiantly.

"*Your* house? You sold it to me three years ago," the man said.

Mike was extremely confused. Sold it? Why?

His entire demeanor changed the moment he realized that things had changed. The guy had to be telling the truth.

"Where do I live now?"

"I have no idea," the man answered.

Mike turned and staggered back towards his car, completely disoriented.

"Are you ok?" the man asked, turning concerned.

Mike didn't answer him as he climbed in. He drove to his parents' house, but no one was home. He then searched for some form of identification that would tell him where he lived, but couldn't find his wallet. He determined it must have fallen into the water when he dove in. He looked in the glove compartment for his insurance card and registration, but both had his old address. He had never been very good about updating information.

A gold band caught his eye on the floor the car. It fit loosely on his wedding finger. Was he married?

He opened his cell phone to check his contacts. He preferred not to sound crazy by asking a friend where he lived, and hoped he had "home" programmed in, and that someone would answer on the other end of the line. Before he could find any numbers, however, the phone turned off. The battery was dead, and IPhone's needed a special charger to charge them in the car. Of course he didn't have one. It took Mike another forty-five minutes just to find a pay phone. He finally found one in front of an old, small-town grocery store that had been there for decades. The phone didn't look a bit out of place.

"I'd like the number for the Mike Postman residence please," he asked the operator.

"That number is unlisted," she responded after a moment.

He must have done that after the insanity of 9/11 he thought to himself. Or maybe to avoid a crazy ex-girlfriend. "Um, I'm...Mike Postman."

"Well, if you're Mike Postman, then you should already know the number," she responded curtly. She would definitely not be getting a quality assurance vote from him.

"Listen. I hit my head, and I can't for the life of me remember my number," Mike tried. "You don't even have to give me the number. Just please connect me to it."

There was a long silence on the other end. Finally, the line began to ring. A little girl answered.

"Postman residence," she said.

"Who's this?" Mike asked.

"It's me, daddy!" the girl answered.

"Who's Me Daddy?" Mike smiled.

"Maaazey," she said, making it sound almost like a question. "When are you coming home?"

"And do you remember where our home is, Mazey, in case you ever get lost?" Mike asked, trying to get the information out of her.

"46 Beach Avenue," she said.

"In what town."

"Woodmont," she answered proudly.

"That's good," Mike said. "Tell your mom I'll be home in a few minutes," and then he wondered exactly who her mother actually was.

He pulled into the driveway of a sprawling

beachfront home with thick white pillars in the front, and a glass wall that encompassed the entire back of the house facing the sound.

The front door flew open and a girl of about four ran down the stone steps and into his arms. He also made out the silhouette of a woman in the doorway, but the floodlights made it impossible to make out much more. He scooped his daughter up with one arm and walked toward the house, stopping when the figure became clearer.

"Kylie," he said at barely above a whisper.

The years had been very kind to her. She had maintained her childhood cuteness, but had added a beauty that came with maturity.

"Where have you been?" she demanded to know.

"I stopped by my parents," he answered.

"They're in Virginia visiting your sister."

"I realized that after I stopped by."

"I've been calling your cell."

"The battery's dead."

"I see you found your wedding ring," she said, softening a little.

"Under the seat in my car," he answered.

"When are you going to get it resized so it stops falling off?"

"I'll do it tomorrow, I promise."

"I was worried about you," she said at last.

"No need to worry about me, babe. I'll always find my way home to you."

He hugged her with his free arm. "God, I've missed you," he said.

"Since this morning?"

"It seems like a lot longer than that," he answered as they went inside.

Almost immediately, there was a knock on the sliding glass door off the living room and a man entered.

"Eddie," Mike said, very surprised to see him. "We do have a front door, ya know."

"I was going for a run on the beach and this was closer," he said. "Hey look, we're thinking about cooking out tomorrow night. You guys in?"

Before Mike could answer, Kylie did. "Definitely. Just don't let Mike near the grill. He burns toast."

"Believe me, I know. I lived with him for seven years," Eddie answered.

Mike followed him out the slider.

"You ok, buddy?" Eddie asked. "You're looking a little pale."

"I'm ok," Mike said unconvincingly. "I've just had a really long five days."

"Well, get inside and be nice to your wife. She was worried, which in turn, got my wife worried, and interrupted the Rangers game."

"Sorry bout that," Mike laughed.

"Who you betting on in the Series?" Eddie asked.

"Not betting this year," Mike answered.

"Not betting?! You've picked ten in a row."

"I don't want to press my luck."

"Well, I guess every streak has to end sometime," Eddie said solemnly. "I like the Cardinals myself. I'll see you tomorrow."

Mike watched Eddie walk across the lawn and

into the equally brilliant house next door. Eddie sold cell phones for a living. Sales must have been very good.

When Kylie fell asleep that night with her head resting comfortably on his chest, Mike decided that what had been his worst day, had now become his favorite. Because of that, and also because he didn't really know what to expect, Mike fought sleep with every ounce of energy he had remaining. Gabriel had never answered what happened at the end of the fifth day.

"Ky. You awake?" he asked, nudging her.

"I am now," she answered, curling up into an even tighter ball next to him.

"There's something I've got to know," he continued.

"What's that?" she groaned.

"You gave up your job at Cantor-Fitzgerald to be a college professor. And I'm a high school teacher."

"Yes."

"And Eddie sells cell phones."

"Correct."

"And his wife is a stay at home mom."

"Correct again. What's your point, Mike?" she said sleepily. "I'm really tired!"

"I'm driving a Porsche and both our families live in million dollar homes. How did that happen?" he asked.

"The Boston Red Sox, babe," she groaned, reluctantly playing along with what she thought was Mike's idea of a joke.

"The Boston Red Sox?"

"Yes, oh all knowing one. But what I'll never

understand," she said, waking up somewhat, "is what ever possessed you to put 50 grand on the series after they fell behind the Yankees three-zip, after already putting 25 grand on them to win the World Series before the season started. Especially when you're a Mets fan."

"Call it a hunch."

"Well, your hunch almost got both Eddie and you divorced. If either of us had known what you were doing ahead of time, we would have killed you."

"Some things you just know, babe," he said with a smile as he kissed her on the forehead.

XVII

~DAY 6 AND BEYOND~

*M*ike was never so happy to wake up at 6:30 in the morning. He opened his eyes, eased his arm out from underneath Kylie, and nearly sprinted for the bathroom. Before he had fallen asleep that night, he had scribbled on his hand in ink. The writing was still fresh. He breathed a deep sigh of relief.

Everything seemed new to him. His car. The drive to work. The rickety old building he worked in. He didn't even mind that most of the male students' boxer shorts were hanging out of the top of their jeans, which fell halfway over their butts.

Mike opened the door to his classroom, and jumped backward. Dozens upon dozens of balloons poured out with literally hundreds more inside. The students in the hallway erupted in laughter.

"Who on earth did that?" a passing teacher asked.

"I think I've got a pretty good idea," Mike answered.

He looked down the corridor and spotted Bill DiPoto. Bill nodded at him in acknowledgement.

As Mike pushed his way into the room, a voice boomed out just above the din, "*WHERE* is all the cafeteria furniture?!!!"

He stuck his head back into the hallway, but this time Bill was nowhere to be found. Mike smiled. For the first time in a long time, he was completely at peace with himself and his life. It wasn't perfect. But his wife was right. It was also far from ordinary.

Heaven could wait for another day.

Acknowledgments

This book came about from a thought that has been rummaging around my mind for a number of years. If I tried to rank them, which would be the best five days of my life? I then developed a story around that question to create "Five Days".

It is a story that has a little bit of everything in it-- romance, friendship, sports, tragedy, heroes, but at its core, its objective is one of reflection. When I think about days from my life, I think about things like my first date (I was in 8th grade and we went roller skating); holidays with my parents and grandparents; scoring the winning goal in the Homecoming soccer game; the first Syracuse football game I ever went to with my dad; graduation nights for both high school and college and all the friends that were a part of both. And of course my wedding day, a day that was like a movie of my life with so many people from so many different parts of it all coming together. I also think about friends and family that I've lost along with events from history I would try to change if I had the opportunity to go back knowing then what I know now. I've incorporated some of those days into this story, leaving one burning question for each reader. Which days would you choose?

Enjoy this book? Turn the page for a preview chapter of another Matt Micros novel; *The Knights of Redemption*...

*T*he Knights of Redemption tells the story of five men who are arrested the same night for unrelated crimes and thrown together in a New Haven, Connecticut jail. Henry Whitman is the President of Yale University who always does the right thing and is the "moral compass" for everyone that knows him. Rogers Conner—the person Major League baseball players voted "the person you would least like to play with"—is about to sign with the Yankees in the twilight of his career. Matt O'Malley is a failed, small-town politician who is trying to pick up the pieces of his career and personal life. Hector Rodriguez is the Assistant Manager at a car wash who has found life in the United States to be a struggle since coming over from Mexico. Mo Falls is a popular television star who has just been thrown off the #1 rated show in the country for his outlandish behavior. At first glance, these men appear to have little in common, but a closer look reveals that their lives are more intertwined than they realize, that they have been brought together for a reason, and that each person— has the ability to help one of the others. Posing the question, "What if you had the opportunity to rectify your greatest mistake?" The Knights of Redemption allows us to reflect on our own successes, failures, and regrets of the past, while gently reminding us that we are given one life to live, so live it well...

THE KNIGHTS OF REDEMPTION

A NOVEL

Matt Micros

For my family and friends...

THE KNIGHTS OF
REDEMPTION

We are all Knights of Redemption. Each possessing the power to listen, learn, teach and inspire...

I.

~HENRY WHITMAN~

*W*hat if everyone's life was judged solely by the worst thing they had ever done? World leaders would no longer be judged by a successful economy or their social programs, but rather, for inappropriate advances on underpaid interns. Professional athletes wouldn't be heroes for hitting 50 home runs or throwing 40 touchdowns in a season, but for refusing to sign an autograph for a ten-year old boy in a wheelchair.

Long before he became President of one of the most prestigious universities in the country, Henry Whitman was a five-year old boy who wrestled his hand from his father's grasp and chased someone two city blocks just to give the man a quarter he had dropped.

When he was ten, he set up a lemonade stand on a street corner with a sign that told customers *exactly* how much each glass had cost him to make, because he didn't want them to feel as though he was unfairly marking the prices up. When he was a senior in high school and was asked to the Sadie Hawkins Spring Fling by two girls—one of them, a sweet, but not entirely attractive oboe player in the band; the other, the captain of the cheerleading squad and a future Miss Connecticut—he went with the oboe player because she had asked him first.

And when his hard working father couldn't afford to send him to college on his factory worker's hourly wage, Henry put himself through by working two jobs and commuting from home to keep the costs down. Once he finally completed his schooling and began bringing home a steady paycheck—it took him nearly ten years to do it--he gave nearly half of it each pay period to his parents because he was grateful they had allowed him to live at home the entire time. He lived by the words of Mark Twain. *"Always do right. It will gratify some people, and astonish the rest."* In fact, it would not be a stretch to say that Henry Whitman made the correct moral and ethical decision in his life every single time--except the one that mattered most.

Henry's first job was as a professor of English at a small, but well-known liberal arts college in Boston. His students loved his classes for he taught them not only an appreciation of literature, but also the crucial life skills of writing and communication. And he did so with an enthusiasm that couldn't possibly have been disingenuous. When they studied Mark Twain, he came to class dressed at Twain. When they studied Fitzgerald, he threw Roaring 20's parties at his house for the entire class and even a few that weren't in it. If students had a problem, whether it be socially, financially or ethically, he was the moral compass they sought out. Which is what made it that much more difficult for them when he was offered to head up the department, and his teaching load was cut in half. He was forced to teach fewer students and had less free time as well. Eventually, he was offered the equivalent position at an even more prestigious college, but when he refused to leave until his current employer had found a suitable replacement for him, he lost out on the other position.

Henry first met his wife at a coffee shop, when he eyed her reading an obscure novel by a long passed away author he admired. He was nearly 40 at the time and said he knew she would be the woman he would marry the moment she peered up at him over the book, her blue eyes looking even larger through a pair of horned rimmed reading glasses. She taught high school freshman English in Watertown, just outside of Boston, but when Henry's parents both grew ill at the same time, he and his wife moved to Connecticut to take care of them and begin a family of their own.

Both had to make sacrifices to do so. Bernadette accepted the only position available to her—a remedial teaching position at a middle school; a job that caused her to literally count down the days to each vacation and the end of the school year. Middle school students were monsters, filled with energy, hormones and a lack of filters that resulted in some of the most outrageous comments coming from their mouths. Her job was living proof that no good deed went unpunished.

Henry fared quite a bit better due to his background and was offered the position of Head of School at Choate. Five years later, he decided he missed being in the classroom and accepted a full-time professorship at nearby Yale. But even though his love was teaching, he kept getting pulled into administration and two months into the school year, he assumed the Department Chair position on an interim basis when the Chair had a stroke. A year later, Henry had the interim tag removed, three years after that, he became the Vice President of Academic Affairs, and five years after that, at age 62, he became President of the University.

He and his wife had two beautiful and well-behaved teenagers (an oxymoron if ever there was one), a nice house in the suburbs, and enough money to live comfortably, if not extravagantly. And then, as if overnight, everything came to pieces one April morning. The thing was, it didn't really happen overnight. Henry had just missed all of the signs.

The day had begun just like any other day. Henry had about a half dozen phone messages and two dozen emails to return, along with responding to three or four invites to university functions that he would need to attend. At 10:00am, he had a meeting with a distinguished alum who was interested in donating a million dollars to help fund building a soccer specific stadium on campus. At 11:30, just as he was about to head out for an early lunch, he received the call. He normally would have let his secretary answer it, but he could see she wasn't at her desk, and he also noticed it was an in-house call, so he grabbed it. Couldn't very well call himself a man of the people, if he wasn't accessible *to* the people.

"Hello," he answered as if he was answering his house phone.

There was silence on the other end of the line for

a moment or two as the person was undoubtedly caught off guard. "Dr. Whitman?" a female answered at last.

"Yes," he said. "How can I help you—" He glanced at the caller ID, "Cheryl is it?"

"Yes," she said. She spoke very quietly, as if she was worried about someone overhearing her. "I was wondering if I could have a few minutes of your time. I normally wouldn't bother you, but I don't know who else to turn to. It's really important."

Henry glanced at his watch, and seemed to be turning over in his mind the effect that an unscheduled meeting would have on the rest of his day, before relenting. "Sure, Cheryl. Come on up. You know where my office is?"

"Yes, I do. Thank you."

Five minutes later, his intercom buzzed. "A Cheryl Rueben is here to see you," his secretary said. "She says you're expecting her?"

"That's right. Send her in."

Cheryl worked for Don Peterson in the fundraising office, working primarily on the Annual Fund. She was young—late twenties maybe—and more sexy than pretty, with a slightly worn appearance the result of living a hard life in her teens. She had worked at Yale for slightly more than three years, but he didn't know much about her other than what he overheard from others. She was a single mother of two little girls to two different fathers, neither of whom she had married. She actually came from old money in Long Island, and had lived a wild life probably in an attempt to rebel against her family as much as anything. Cheryl had attended nearby Poquonic College, known for being a country club type refuge for the tri-state area student who didn't want an education to interfere with their social life. After graduation, she worked as an intern in the development office at Poquonic for a few years, before coming to Yale. How she landed her current position was a mystery to most, but she did her job, and Henry hadn't received any complaints about her, so he didn't ask many questions. He trusted that Don knew what he was doing, as evidenced by an ever-burgeoning endowment.

"What can I do for you, Cheryl?" Henry asked curiously. Rarely did he allow himself to take a meeting without being properly prepared first.

"I'm not sure how to begin," she stammered, a bit overwhelmed now that she found herself face to face with the most powerful man in arguably the most powerful university in the country.

"Begin by just telling me what's on your mind."

She paused for a moment before beginning. "I was really excited when I got this job. I meet interesting people every day. I get to go to great events..."

"But..."

"I'm being harassed by Don Peterson," she blurted out at last.

"What do you mean by harassed? Yelled at for your work?"

"Sexually harassed."

"By Don?" he asked incredulously.

"It started shortly after I started working for him. Emails at first, telling me what to wear to department meetings. Low-cut tops, short skirts, stiletto heels. I thought he was joking, but then he started refusing to sign off on my vacation days, even though I had some coming. Eventually, he started calling me late at night, saying sexually explicit things and demanding phone sex, so he could—this is really uncomfortable for me," she said, stopping herself short.

"I don't mean this to sound insensitive, but did you in any way, even inadvertently, give him any indication it was reciprocal? Don't get me wrong. He's married and it would still be wrong, but I'm just trying to understand it because it sounds so out of character for the Don I know."

She thought about it for a moment before answering. "I've wondered that same thing for a long time, but the answer is no. I would tell him I was going to sleep. I even stopped answering the phone."

"And did it stop?"

"It got worse. He would berate me in front of the others. Then he started demanding oral sex or he'd fire me."

"When?! Where?!"

"In his office. He'd lock the door and close the blinds. But everyone knew what was going on. It was mortifying."

She was crying now.

"That was my next question. Who else knows about this?"

"The other men in the office," she sniffled. "Because he told them they could run the train on me."

"I don't know what that means," Henry said.

"One of them would have sex with me from behind, while I was forced to give oral sex to the other."

The immortal words of Gary Coleman in *Different Strokes* came immediately to mind. *"Whatchu talkin bout Willis?"* Henry had lived a pretty sheltered life, and this was an area he had very little experience in. He was mortified, but decided to try and stick just with the facts.

"Do you have any emails or texts from him?" he asked.

"He makes me delete them all. He stands right over me while I do it."

"I see."

She was sensing that he didn't believe her. "I know this is all pretty difficult to believe. But it's true. Every word of it. And the only reason I didn't come forward sooner is because I really need this job. I'm a single mother, trying to raise two kids. My parents cut me off long ago when I made some poor decisions."

"Is there anyone else who can corroborate your story? Anyone at all?"

"There are others. They've never said anything to me, but I can tell."

"How can you tell?"

"Because they have the same look on their face that I see every time I look in the mirror."

"Do you think any of them would speak up?"

"I doubt it."

Henry walked across the room. Poured himself a glass of Scotch. It was a little early in the day, but if ever there was something that warranted it, this was it. "You do realize without any proof or any other people backing up your story, it will be difficult to do anything about this."

"I know, but I had to say something."

"I'll look into it," Henry promised. "But understand, as soon as I do, you could get some pushback. And I can't do anything about that without proof. So what I'd do in the meantime, is get some proof."

Cheryl nodded a disappointed nod and let herself out. The moment she left his office, a hundred thoughts competed for a place within his mind. On one hand, Don Peterson appeared to be a family man. Married for more than twenty years with three children, he coached his son's little league baseball team and his wife was by his side for every Yale function. On the other, was that Henry had always found him to be a bit of a slickster—part corporate executive fundraiser, part used car salesman, complete with the jet black, slicked back hair. Another red flag should have been the turnover within his department since taking over five years ago. When he began the job, he had seven men and three women working under him, with an average age of somewhere in the vicinity of fifty years old. Now there were seven *women,* all extremely attractive, and just three men working there with an average age that couldn't have been even thirty. Henry had chalked it up to a natural turnover that occurred whenever you had an older staff to begin with, plus his new staff had been extremely successful. The Yale endowment had never been higher.

He decided to meet individually with the other

members of the department to see what they knew, but if they knew anything, they weren't saying.

Don himself simply stated, "She's just pissed because I refused her vacation time two days before our big gala dinner dance because there was a ton of work that needed to be done. As you know, it's the biggest event of the year and we needed all hands on deck. She wanted to go to Cabo with a few of her friends. Anyway, she's been pissed off ever since."

It sounded plausible. Don had a way of making anything seem plausible. Which was probably also why he was so good at his job.

"Do you recall ever saying anything that she could have misconstrued as being sexual in nature?"

"Absolutely not."

"What about telling her what to wear into the office?"

"If anything, I tell them all to tone it down a bit. Some of them, her in particular, tend to dress like they're going clubbing."

Still not completely satisfied, Henry sought out someone in the computer technology department. Stephen Schuler had worked there for a little over three months, but had quickly gained Henry's trust. He was sharp, reliable and discreet.

"Schu, is it possible to retrieve someone's work email even if it's been deleted?" Henry asked.

"Yes, but I'd need the actual computer to do it."

Since Don always took his laptop home with him at the end of a day, anything that was going to be done needed to be done *during* the day. While Henry took Don to lunch one afternoon, Schuler cloned Don's computer and swapped it out with the original, so he could have enough time to thoroughly search the hard drive. Don would be none the wiser.

Two days later, Schu walked into Henry's office with a memory stick. "You're not going to like what I found," he said.

On the stick were hundreds of emails, mostly graphic in nature, covering not only what to wear to work, but how nice certain body parts of hers looked. And they weren't just to her, but to several, if not all of the other female members of the office as well. It was more of a smoking gun than O.J. racing down the 405 Freeway in his Ford Bronco.

It left Henry with four choices to choose from. Ignore it, and hope the girl eventually quit. With no evidence to support her claims, she would have a difficult time proving anything. But heaven forbid she could...

He could offer to buy her silence by paying her off with a confidentiality clause that would prevent her from talking about it to anyone. Since she needed the money, this was an appealing option, although getting approval from the Board of Directors without a proper explanation, might be a bit tricky.

He could fire Don on the spot. But that would likely result in a very ugly, very public mess that the media would pounce on. The statement that "there's no such thing as bad publicity" did not apply to institutions of higher learning.

He could force Don into an early retirement. That wouldn't be easy to do since Don was only 51, but looking at a nice severance package, and a reference for future employment while staring at a memory card full of evidence, might be enough to coerce him to go away quietly. But if it wasn't, things could get ugly.

"What do you want me to do, Dr. Whitman?" Schuler asked.

"Is this the only copy?" was Henry's response.

"Yes."

"Well, I guess there's only one thing *to* do. I'll take care of it, Schu. Thanks."

Henry sat motionless at his desk after Schuler left, holding the memory stick in front of him with both hands for five or ten seconds, before snapping it in two and throwing it into the garbage.

That night as he and his wife prepared for bed, his doorbell rang. Henry answered it in his bathrobe and was greeted by two uniformed police officers. "Can I help you?" he asked.

"Dr. Whitman?" one of the officers asked.

"Yes?"

"We have a warrant for your arrest."